# Gentle Hearts, Guilty Sins

To Noble
my old friend
Maggie Morgan Doran '03

# Gentle Hearts, Guilty Sins

by

Maggie Morgan Doran

TripleTree Publishing
Eugene Oregon

ISBN: 0-9716638-3-1

Library of Congress #2002109712

 "End October" originally appeared in the *Chaminade Literary Review* "Billy and Benjamin Too" originally appeared in *Dead on Demand—the Best of Ghost Story Weekend.*

TripleTree Publishing
PO Box 5684, Eugene, OR 97405
(541) 338-3184 – www.TripleTreePub.com

Cover watercolor by Maggie Morgan Doran
Cover and interior design by Alan M. Clark
Printed in the United States of America
1 2 3 4 5 6 7 8 9

This collection of stories is dedicated to
Russ, Diane, and Julie,
in appreciation of their enduring encouragement
and faith.


## Acknowledgements

Finally, here in my seventy-fifth year, I have the opportunity to thank Liz Cratty for her professional guidance, for her always-to-the-point criticism, and for the soft pressure that kept me going. More than that, I want to thank her for our friendship over the decades, over great distances, and across generations. Also, let me thank Van and Dan, Sandy, Joyce, and every one of my extensive and extended family scattered about the world.

# Table of Contents

# The Estate of Joseph P. Bosley

THURMAN

There were thirteen people at Ol' Joe Bosley's funeral. Eleven brothers from the Eagles Lodge 626, The Kid, and a lady. It was the last one who caused Thurman's jaw to go slack as he watched her get out of Buzz's Taxi at the cemetery. Buzz had pulled in behind the Barstow's Mortuary Buick then got out and taken a big scarred-up old suitcase out of the trunk before he opened the back door and helped her out. If Thurman had been given to fancy phrases, he would have said she defied description. What he did say, under his breath, was, "Jesus, my all!"

From his position at a discreet distance from the little group that occupied the row of folding chairs at the graveside, Thurman glanced over at Bill Barstow and Reverend Arbuckle and could tell from their faces that they didn't know who she was. Reverend Arbuckle looked shocked and Bill looked like he didn't know whether to go out there and talk to her, or stay where he was, or what the hell to do. All kinds of weird people came to funerals, for all kinds of crazy reasons. That was one thing Thurman had learned since he started helping out at Barstow's, and this one was about the weirdest.

Bill must have made up his mind finally because he walked over by the taxi where the lady was standing, looking like she was no more sure of herself than he was, and said something to her. She mumbled an answer and he put his arm under her elbow, walked her slowly in front of the Eagles and The Kid, and seated her in the one remaining chair at the far end of the row.

Thurman truly tried not to stare and to tend to his business which was to watch and be ready in case any of the loved ones needed his assistance. Even so, his gaze kept running down the row of Eagles, over the top of The Kid's head and getting stuck on the lady. He couldn't get over her. She was as big a woman as he'd ever seen. Not just fat, though it was easy to see she had put away her share of mashed potatoes and gravy, but *big*, maybe six foot. Even sitting down, her head was higher than anybody else's. And her hair was the damnedest color.

Again Thurman turned his head away, but his eyes automatically moved sideways in their sockets to look at her. It was like she was the only thing out there. You didn't see Reverend Arbuckle, The Kid, the Eagles, Joe's casket or anything else, Thurman thought. Just her.

It wasn't only her build that was unusual, it was the way she was dressed, too. Thurman's wife, Eula, once had a blouse she got at LaMode's that was the color of the dress the lady had on. Eula had called it "electric blue" and she told Thurman when she brought it home that it was a very popular color that year. It was exactly the same blue of the dress the lady had on, but Thurman thought it must have been made out of a different kind of material. This lady's dress had to be out of some stretchy stuff because she was packed into it like sausage into pig gut. It swelled out like big blue balloons where her bosom rose, where her belly billowed onto her lap, and where her thighs bulged over the sides of the chair. Filled up the way it was, there wasn't enough left of the dress to cover the lady's knees, and again Thurman turned his eyes away. But in his mind he could see her legs and they made him think of giant chicken drumsticks: big at the knee where her nylons were stretched and shiny in the sun, they puffed out at the calves and narrowed down to nice ankles. She had on high-heeled black patent pumps and she had worked the heel strap of one of them down to take the pressure off.

Thurman made another half-hearted attempt to get his attention off of her, but gave up and let his gaze, which had made its way down the lady's form, start back up. It hesitated at her hands which were clamped over the top of a black purse with a sparkly clasp on it, and went on to her face. He judged her to be fifty or more, and she had one of those big open faces that age doesn't wrinkle so much as it just lets it loose to hang in fleshy bags and pouches. It was hot in the cemetery, and the lady's forehead was shiny with sweat. The skin under her heavy black-penciled eyebrows had begun to hang down over her eyes a little, and there was a series of bags underneath, draped like the ivory-colored valance above the curtain on the high school stage. Her nose was crowded between cheeks flushed with rouge and the heat of the afternoon.

She raised her head and Thurman quickly dropped his, but then when he was sure she had lowered hers, he looked back and that time he decided that maybe she had once been pretty and he felt bad for her. But then he looked at her mouth and he could see that the years hadn't made it tighten up. It was big, and the full lips, even though they were covered with a thick coat of red-orange lipstick, had an easy, comfortable look. He hid a little grin. There was a mouth that liked to laugh. He didn't feel so bad for her then.

Finally Thurman focused his attention on her hair. He had never seen hair that color. First he thought it was red, then he thought it was blonde. Whatever color it was, Thurman knew for sure that it was the prettiest hair he had ever seen. Wavy and soft-looking, it made a red-gold mist around the lady's sweaty face. On top of it she had pinned a little bit of a hat with a wad of net on it, but you could hardly see it because of the way the hair fluffed out. It occurred to Thurman, who seldom gave any thought to how women feel, that if the only beautiful part of a woman was her hair, she sure wouldn't cover it up with a big hat.

Well, she was no beauty. Of all the unlikely people he'd seen at funerals, this one got the prize. But long experience had taught him there's no explaining people. You just live your life and let them live theirs, and that way you stay out of trouble.

Thurman moved his weight from one foot to the other, folded his arms across his chest and reminded himself of where he was and the nature of his responsibilities. He made himself listen respectfully to Reverend Arbuckle. The minister had four or five sermons for funerals, and mostly he just changed the names. He was good at it, though, and Thurman had never yet caught him in a mistake. This was Number Four, the one he used for men he didn't know, or ones there wasn't much to say about.

Joe Bosley fit naturally into the last group. Reverend Arbuckle was droning..."a quiet and unassuming man"...and Thurman couldn't help thinking that Joe had had a lot to be unassuming about. He had never done much that amounted to anything except to take in The Kid. And he really hadn't even taken her in. When his no-account daughter who had had the baby but no husband, had walked out, leaving no forwarding address, Joe didn't have much choice about keeping The Kid.

To be fair, though, Joe had done the best he could, given that they had to live on his disability pension and a few pissant handyman jobs people around town gave him out of pity for the little girl. She looked healthy enough, and had warm clothes when she played outside in the winter. And he had put her in kindergarten when she was five.

Another thing. Joe had kept the house up so they had a nice place to live. Nothing fancy, but he took good care of it. Thurman knew, because he had passed Joe's house at least once a day for more years than he could remember. Joe's place was between his own house and the two blocks of stores and offices that made up the town's so-called business district. If Thurman hadn't passed Joe's on the way to work, then he had on the way to the Safeway or the Post Office. Keeping your place up was important around there, and Joe had done as well as the rest of them. He painted the house every four or five years and last year he had put on a new composition roof. Every spring he cut back the branches of the weeping willow in the front yard and he kept the grass mowed. When The Kid was two or three years old, he had built a nice picket fence and painted it white like the house. Then about the time she started to school, Thurman had seen the Sears truck unload a whole set of new bathroom fixtures—toilet, sink and bathtub—in the driveway. Thurman had stopped and asked Joe if he could use some help, and Joe had acted like he was glad to get it. The inside of the house was plain, as Thurman remembered, but clean.

What Thurman couldn't see with his own eyes as he passed Joe's place every day, he heard about at the hardware store or the Orange Owl where he went for coffee. Nobody had any secrets in that town. And that's the way it ought to be, Thurman thought. Nothing keeps people honest and upstanding better than having everybody else know what they're doing all the time.

As for The Kid, Thurman had watched her playing in the yard or walking to school since she was a baby. She was as skinny as a maple switch, but Thurman knew, from raising four of his own, that lots of kids were just skinny at that age, and there wasn't anything you could do about it. They stayed skinny even if they ate like horses. Of course, Joe had always bought The Kid's clothes three sizes too big, according to Eula, and that made her look even skinnier.

There she sat, little and pitiful, between Arnold Ledbetter in his Eagles uniform, and the big lady. It wasn't that the little girl was ugly, she was just plain. Her hair was what Eula called dishwater blonde, and she had pulled it back on both sides from a ragged part and pinned it with bobby pins. The worst thing, and the thing that made you think at first that she was ugly, was that hang-dog look she always had about her.

Joe and The Kid kept to themselves. Once in a while he went to Lodge meeting, and he was at the lumber yard and the hardware store fairly regularly. Sometimes he took her with him when he went to the Safeway, and when he did odd jobs around town. Thurman had seen her sitting in the car, waiting for him. Generally, though, they just stayed around the place. Except on Sunday nights when Joe went to his brother's place in Junction City and stayed over. Then he always got Pearl, the Pruitt's daughter, to come over and stay with the girl. Pearl never was very bright, but she knew enough to see that nothing happened to The Kid. And Joe was always home on Monday before The Kid got in from school.

The only thing that bothered Thurman about Joe going off to his brother's was that he never took the girl. Of course, he'd been doing that—going off to Junction City—for twenty years, long before the girl was born, so it was understandable. Still, you'd think that when she was a baby he'd have taken her to show her off. Thurman figured that the brother or his wife probably didn't approve of The Kid because of where she came from. Some people were like that. Maybe that was why they hadn't bothered to come to the funeral. There weren't even any flowers for Ol' Joe, except the standard Everlasting Bouquet of blue chrysanthemums from the Eagles Lodge.

He looked at The Kid again and shook his head. He felt so damned sorry for the little thing. Never had a chance and now she never would. Now the county would probably pay some sorry family sixty dollars a month to take her in where she could help with the chores.

AMBER JEAN

The Kid squirmed on her chair and put her hand to her mouth to chew at a fingernail. Then she remembered she wasn't supposed to, and took it away, wiping the back of her hand across her mouth. She felt all tight and shaky inside. Pulling herself up straight, she leaned forward and gripped the sides of the metal chair with both hands and brought her feet up to press her heels hard against the underside of the seat. Then she fumbled into her dress pocket to make sure she hadn't lost her key. Then she pulled up her socks.

Reverend Arbuckle glanced at her with the kind of a look that means, *sit still,* but she was too excited.

She'd had two *best* days in her life, and this was the second one. The first one was when she started to school. Not the first day *of* school, but the day Joe took her over to the school so he could write his name on some papers and give them some money.

Since it had been her first best day, she remembered everything about it. They had gone into a room with four yellow wood chairs and a high counter and there was a lady with blue hair behind it. A mother whose boy was sucking his finger and leaning against her was at the counter and the lady with the blue hair was talking to her. There were three other people, a man, a woman, and a little girl, sitting in the chairs. She and Joe just stood around for awhile, till finally the man leaned down and whispered something to his little girl and she got on his lap. Then there were two empty chairs so she and Joe sat down.

After a while, the lady and the boy sucking his finger left, and the man, woman, and the little girl went up to the counter. When the lady was through with them, she made a quick smile and looked at Joe and said, "Mr. Bosley?" and Joe had got up. He didn't take hold of her hand or anything, but she had known she was supposed to go with him.

The counter was too high for her to see what was going on, but she heard the lady ask a question. Joe didn't answer for a second and then he said, "Amber Jean Bosley."

She remembered looking straight up at Joe because she wasn't sure she had heard him right. And the lady must not have heard him right, either, because she said, "Pardon?" and Joe said, "Amber Jean Bosley," as plain as day.

That was the first time she ever knew she had a whole

name like that, with three parts. She remembered that once when she was sick Joe took her to the clinic and the nurse called her *Jean*, but Joe never called her that. He didn't call her anything. But that was all right because there was never anybody else around anyway. So, if he talked, she knew he was talking to her. And then, if they were over at the Safeway, he might say—when the girl who took the money tried to joke around—that he was getting something for The Kid. Or The Girl.

It was plain to her that up to the time she had to go to school, that she hadn't needed a regular three-part name, and then when she did, it turned out to be the most beautiful name she had ever heard. All the way home she had said it over and over again to herself. As soon as they got there, she changed her dress as fast as she could and then went out in the yard, under the willow tree, and practiced saying it out loud. After a while she had gone back into the house to the bathroom and pulled the dirty clothes hamper over under the sink and stood on it so she could see in the mirror. Then she said her name more times, low, so Joe couldn't hear it in the kitchen where he was frying hot dogs for their supper. She looked at herself and turned her head from side to side and thought about how people could say to one another, "There goes Amber Jean Bosley. My, isn't she a nice little girl. Such a pretty name, too." She could imagine several ladies standing outside the post office as she and Joe walked by, and saying that to one another.

That was the first best day of her life. And today would be the second. It just *had* to be. All the time at Barstow's Funeral Home when the organ music was playing, she had kept looking back at the door, waiting. But nobody had come. For a while she was afraid she had got it wrong. That she had misunderstood what Joe had told her. But that couldn't be. It just couldn't. She remembered exactly what he said.

It was before supper one day. Joe had got up and turned off the TV and she thought he was going outside to work in the yard, but instead he sat back down in his chair, and not looking at her, told her he wasn't going to be around much longer. He didn't say anything more for a long time, just sat there looking at the floor. She didn't know what he meant, but she had a bad feeling in her stomach and for that reason, decided not to ask.

Finally he looked at her and asked if she remembered the cat they had, named Blackie, and she did. Then he said did she remember that Blackie had died, and they put him in a garbage bag and took him out to the country and buried him in the ground. She said yes.

He didn't go on, so she just stood there, looking at the green squares in the linoleum, and finally she went outside. She got under the willow tree, way back on the far side where the branches hung to the ground and made a cave, and stayed there till the sun went down.

It had been a day or two after that when Joe said she ought not to worry about anything, that he had someone to come and live in the house with her. She waited for him to tell her something more, but he didn't. Then, one night, just after the news, she asked him who, and he told her to turn the TV down—so she knew that what he was going to say would be all right. If it was going to be as bad as that other time, he would have asked her to turn it off.

Amber Jean could remember how Joe's face looked different when he told her about the lady who was going to come there and live with her. She just couldn't quit looking at him because his face made her feel so good. He said that the lady would be real nice to her, and that she was a good cook. He said he had known her a long time and they had lots of good times together, and that she needed a place to live.

After that, Amber Jean began to take a lot more notice of the women she saw walking by the house and at the Safeway. And also the teachers and the mothers who came to school once in a while. Even so, she could never get a clear picture of what she expected the lady to look like. But, after giving it a lot of thought, she decided what she *didn't* want her to be. Not old, like Reverend Arbuckle's mother because they had to push her around in a wheelchair and she had knobs on her hands; not young like the girl at the post office who was so snippy and didn't know anything about anything. (More times than once she had put the wrong mail in their box, and once she gave their water bill to Mrs. Johnson.)

And she didn't want her to be all skin and bones because all of the skinny women she could think of—Mrs. Wilson, the third grade teacher, and Mrs. Pruitt, Pearl's mother, and some others, too, were always cranky. All Mrs. Pruitt ever did was holler at Pearl and complain about everything. And besides, there was a fat lady who sat on a chair on her porch and smiled and waved at Amber Jean when she went by on her way to school. It seemed like there might be a connection between skinny and cranky, and between fat and nice.

Just then Amber Jean heard the gravel on the road popping and she looked over and there was Buzz's Taxi stopping behind the black car they had brought her out to the cemetery in. At first she didn't think much about it, but suddenly her heart started to pound. She twisted in her chair and tried to raise her head higher to get a better look.

It was her! She just knew it. The lady Joe told her about was in that taxi! She swallowed and stretched her neck around farther.

Amber Jean's breathing stopped as she watched Buzz get out of the taxi, go around and take a suitcase out of the trunk and set it beside the road. Her hands were two little hard fists as he opened the back door. She heard herself gasp and clamped her hand over her mouth.

The lady standing beside Buzz's Taxi looked like a fairy godmother! Amber Jean had never pictured anything so wonderful. She was beautiful—like a fairyland queen that was in a book at school. Amber Jean rubbed her eyes and looked again. A fairy godmother. She kept repeating the words to herself. There she stood, tall and not the least bit skinny, in a dress of the most beautiful blue Amber Jean had ever seen. There was a glow around her face, just like a fairy godmother ought to have. Then, all of a sudden, she figured it out—it was the lady's hair that made her seem to glow. It was like angel's hair under the Christmas tree at school. Like a reddish-golden cloud at sunset. No! Like a fairy godmother's crown of gold!

Amber Jean gripped the back of the chair to lift herself higher. She swallowed and felt her heart thumping. The lady hadn't even looked in her direction. She watched Mister Barstow go over to her and say something, and then put his hand under her elbow and start toward them.

As they came near, the lady reached up and adjusted her little black hat and Amber Jean saw jewels sparkle on her fingers. She shivered with happiness and remembered how Joe's face had looked different when he talked about this lady. In her chest there was a feeling of something good, like butter, or Hershey bars, melting. When Mister Barstow seated the lady in the chair beside Amber Jean, she felt like a million balloons ready to bust loose and fly into the sky.

She didn't dare look up right then because she had another strange new feeling—that she might cry, even though she had never been so happy, not even on her first best day. Her hands felt wet in the palms and her feet kept twisting around each other. Out of the corner of her eye she could see the lady's hands with their shining rings and long orange-colored fingernails, and Amber Jean tucked her own ragged fingertips under her thighs and promised herself she would never again chew them.

Amber Jean held herself in tight so she wouldn't wiggle anymore, but it seemed like Reverend Arbuckle would talk forever. Something told her she ought to be listening to him, so she tried, but it was hard. He was saying, "Joe was a quiet...", then some word she didn't know..."man." She wondered if the preacher was saying something nice or something bad. She thought it was probably supposed to be nice. It was true that Joe was quiet. He just fixed their food and cleaned up the place, and they would watch TV. When he went around town to do some painting or put a new storm door on somebody's house, he would have her take her Cinderella color book and her Crayolas, and she would sit in the back of the car, sometimes a whole afternoon. Once in a while he would come and see if she needed to go to the bathroom. Sometimes he would take her to the bathroom inside the house where he was working, if nobody was home, but lots of times he would have to drive all the way home and back just because she had to go. But he never got mad at her.

Amber Jean was sorry Joe died. But after he told her he was going to, she got used to the idea. She didn't even cry when Reverend Arbuckle came to the Pruitt's where she had been staying since they took Joe to the hospital, and said Joe had passed on. One reason was at first she didn't know what "passed on" meant, but later she did. She had thought about what they would do with him and wondered whether they put dead people in garbage bags. At the funeral home when she looked in the casket, she could see there wasn't any garbage bag, but she didn't think that was really Joe, anyway. Just a dummy made up to look like him. She guessed they did that because people wouldn't want to look at someone they loved after they were dead.

Joe had died just like he said he would, and he had told her it was all worked out, too, so she didn't need to worry about anything. And now, after seeing the fairy godmother, she knew everything would be perfect. She wrapped her arms around herself and hugged tight.

Her heart had almost settled down once, but it was beating hard again. She wanted so bad to look up at her fairy godmother there beside her, but she felt funny. Not exactly scared, but maybe a little, because it seemed too good to be true. She kept wondering what would happen if she looked right up at the lady, and finally she decided she would have to, or die.

Very slowly she raised her head and found herself staring right into the lady's eyes. A big, hard knob swelled up in her throat and she wanted, more than she had ever wanted anything in her whole life, to put her arms around the lady's neck and lay her head against her. She looked so big and soft and kind.

Then she saw tears fill the lady's eyes and Amber Jean was suddenly embarrassed and scared. Quickly she turned away and looked down at the ground in front of her. Frantically she thought, "Why is she crying? Doesn't she like me?"

Amber Jean sat absolutely still, folding her hands together and then straightening them out again, a terrible tightness in her chest and tears pressing against the backs of her eyeballs. Finally, when the pain wasn't so bad, she tried to think straight like Joe had always told her to. She remembered the exact moment her eyes met the lady's, and she knew the lady *did* like her. The happiness that had shrunk to a little tiny peanut size in her stomach began to get big again and push everything else out.

The lady liked her. She knew it. She ached to talk to her and searched into all the corners of her head for something to say. She thought about saying right out, "You look like a fairy godmother," but that didn't seem right. Nothing did. She pulled her dress far down over her knees and fidgeted with the key in her pocket.

After a long time, she sighed, discouraged. If I just knew her name, she thought, I'd ask her if I could borrow a Kleenex.

## NELLIE

Nellie was hot. Sitting at the end of the row of chairs, she got the afternoon sun full on her. Her feet hurt in her sling pumps and her girdle was cutting into her stomach and crotch.

What was bothering her more, though, was that she was disgusted with that little poop of a preacher. Look at him, she thought, standing up there as pious as J. C. Himself, acting like Joe had been his best friend when he didn't know diddly squat about him. Hell, it sounded like the sermon was written for just anybody, with Joe's name plugged in here and there. Joe had been too decent a guy to have some two-faced little twit make up a bunch of crap about him.

She shifted her weight on the folding metal chair and dug in her purse for a Kleenex. Stretching her neck forward, she dabbed at it and wished the whole thing was over. Wearily she folded her hands in her lap over the mint green tissue and looked into the big rectangular hole in front of her where they would put Joe's casket. When she thought about them shoveling dirt in on him, her eyes stung. She swallowed at a pain in her throat.

What a shame. Life hadn't been a rose garden for Joe. Still, in their way, they'd had some good years. She lowered her head and ran her hand along the back of her neck, lifting the soft curls just enough to let the air cool her damp skin. Yes, they'd had some *damned* good years. Joe had been the best friend a woman ever had, and, for a long time, the best lover, too. And he always made her laugh. They hadn't stopped laughing, not even in the last year when they both knew their time was running out. Sunlight danced on a large red glass stone in one of her rings as she raised her hand and delicately pressed the damp tissue against first her left, then her right nostril.

Breathing a long sigh, she raised her head and let one side of her wide mouth lift in a sad little smile. One night a week for twenty years. That's all they'd had. But every one had been a good one.

They had a routine, she and Joe did. Joe would show up with the beer and they would sit down at her Formica kitchen table beside the window and drink it while they told each other any jokes they had heard during the week, and went over anything else that had happened. Once they got caught up she would get supper on the table while they finished off the beer. Later he would help her with the dishes, and that's when they would begin to pat and nuzzle and rub against each other, so when the last pan was dried and put away, they would be dying to get into bed. Nellie squirmed on her chair, remembering.

Afterward, they would have a cigarette, and that was an old movie joke that always made them laugh. The rest of the night they would talk and giggle and take time out for a good hump whenever they felt like it. They were like two sixteen-year-old kids with the hots for each other, right up to the time he couldn't do anything anymore. Even then, they would climb into bed when the dishes were done and talk and laugh the night through.

In the early years Nellie had tried to get Joe to come to Junction City and move in with her, but he always hung back. Then after a time, she began to think that it wouldn't be the same if they lived together. There wasn't any married couple she knew who got along like she and Joe did.

A fly settled on Nellie's cheek and she brushed it away. The preacher was saying... "a quiet and unassuming man".... Oh, no! Not *her* Joe. But, then she had always known that Joe was a different guy when he was with her at her apartment. When she first knew him, when he was a once-a-week customer at the cafe where she worked, he was a real dud. Even when he had asked her out for a beer, he had been so quiet she about gave up on him.

But, then, one night she took him home with her, and it seemed like when there wasn't anyone else around he could let go. There, in her two-room upstairs apartment, he had been the talkingest, funniest guy she'd ever been around.

That first time was it. After that, she never even thought about anybody else. Joe was her man and she didn't need to know where he spent the other six nights a week to know that she was his woman. He always acted like the only thing he saw was her hair, and every Sunday, when she heard him coming up the wooden stairway and went to open the door, he would raise his hand and stroke the curls softly back from her face, then pat her hair and kiss her. It was just his way to ignore her size and a face that had seen better days. Occasionally she wondered how he could love a big cow like her, but she never wondered *if* he did. She knew. Nellie lifted her eyebrows sadly, pulled her mouth in at the corners and sniffed quietly.

They had never talked about his trouble. Once, when she first noticed that he was losing weight, she asked him if he had been to the doctor and he had frowned and said yes and then got up and went to the fridge for another beer. She knew two things right then—that he wasn't going to talk about it, and that he was going to die. When he left that time she gave way and bawled for three days. But then she decided that when you've only got one night a week, you don't waste it pissing and moaning about something you can't change.

She never mentioned it again. But, then, a couple of months ago, Joe brought it up, in a way, himself. What he said was that he had brought some papers with him that he wanted her to sign. Then he went into a long explanation about how he had known she was strapped for money. He had been embarrassed, bringing it out in the open like that, and Nellie had been embarrassed, too, because she had tried so hard to hide it from him.

He knew, of course, that she had had to quit work after she had three blood clots in her leg in one month. She had thought her second husband's vet's pension would be enough to get by on. The fact was that it didn't even come close, and it had taken her only about six months to go through what little savings she had. She had cut down every place she could. Then her rent went up thirty dollars a month, and every time she went to the store, it seemed to cost her more. She knew when Joe caught on, because he started bringing a ham or a can of coffee whenever he came, and finally he would show up with a big bag of groceries every week. She'd say he didn't need to do that, and he'd turn away and sorta wave his hand around like he didn't know what to say.

They had been lying in bed when Joe said that about the papers he wanted her to sign. At first she didn't understand, but finally it sunk in that he was signing his house over to her. She was so taken back tht she hadn't been able to think straight and in her confusion she missed part of what he was saying. Then she realized he was telling her that she would have to share it with The Kid. He said he was sorry about that, but it was the only way he could think of to be sure both of them would be taken care of.

Nellie sniffed as she thought that was just like Joe. There the man was dying and all he was thinking about was how to be sure two females who didn't have any legal claim on him would be taken care of when he was gone. Nellie hadn't known what to say that night, so she hadn't said anything, just put her big arm around him and pulled his head over on her shoulder.

After he went to sleep, she gave it some thought. She had never seen the little girl or the house, but up till then it hadn't mattered. Joe talked a lot about his house, about painting it, putting in the new bathroom, and all the other repairs and remodeling he did on it.

But the little girl. Now that was something different. It wasn't like he didn't care about her. More like the whole thing had him buffaloed. So when he did talk about her, it was just to say she was all right. Oh, maybe he would tell Nellie about buying the girl a new winter coat, or teaching her to make the beds. And he had mentioned several times that she was real quick to learn. The only time he had ever said anything sweet was when she started to school, and he had told Nellie that she looked pretty as a picture in her new outfit. He'd looked a little embarrassed, but proud, too.

The morning after Joe mentioned the papers, they had gone down to the notary public so she could sign them, and on the way back he told her that he'd done some checking and found out that a percentage of his disability pension could go to the girl when he was gone. Then, with Nellie's second husband's pension, he thought the two of them could get along fine. She would own the house free and clear, and he had the repairs all up so it wouldn't need any money spent on it for a few years. He reminded her that she'd have to put a little aside every month to pay the taxes. Remembering it, Nellie thought for a minute she was going to break down. Good old Joe. She pulled in a deep breath, swallowed, and sat up straight. She didn't want to go to pieces in front of all these strangers.

Strangers? What about The Kid? Well, it was the truth. Even though they were going to share Joe's house, they were still strangers. Nellie hadn't even looked closely at the girl. The only impression she had was that she was skinny and her dress was two or three sizes too big.

Nellie turned her head just enough to look down at the

little figure beside her. The Kid's head was bowed, her hands in her lap. She had pulled her dark blue print dress modestly over her knees, but her skinny legs hung out. Her hair was a mess, stringy and dull, but Nellie thought a lemon rinse would make a world of difference. The elastic was gone out of the girl's socks and they fell in folds over the tops of her tennis shoes. As Nellie watched, the child put a finger in her mouth and began to gnaw at a fingernail already chewed to the quick.

The gesture cut straight into Nellie. Suddenly she wanted to lift the skinny kid on her lap and hold her close. Poor little snot, she thought. Poor little thing.

She was still looking down at the girl when all at once she raised her head and looked directly into Nellie's eyes. What Nellie saw in the thin face was something she never could have imagined in a million years. She sucked in her breath, and in spite of herself, pulled away slightly. The child's face was glowing with love.

In that moment, Nellie felt all the heaviness of her whole life lift. Tears began to run down her face. She reached out her hand, but the little girl, abashed by the tears, once again had dropped her head and was nervously working her hands in her lap.

Nell was overcome. When they had looked into each other's eyes, she had known she loved this kid. Joe's granddaughter. She dabbed at her eyes, and though she was not a religious woman, she raised her face to the sky in a kind of prayer.

Wiping at her nose with her Kleenex, she leaned down to speak to the little girl. She opened her mouth, then hesitated. Abruptly she turned in her chair and stared straight ahead.

"Good God," she breathed, "I don't even know her name."

## THURMAN

When it hit Thurman he was just suppressing a yawn,

his nostrils hard and white. His head snapped around so he could see the big lady at the end of the row, and before he got ahold of himself, the yawn which had stopped in mid-gape, got mixed up with the need to laugh, and he snorted loudly. Catching Reverend Arbuckle's peevish glance, he ducked his head, put his hand over his mouth and pretended he was coughing.

Hell, he said to himself, that lady is Joe's brother! For God's sake, that's where Ol' Joe went every Sunday...to see that woman!

He rubbed his nose with his handkerchief, but his shoulders continued to shake. He couldn't help it. W'y that old dog. He's had a woman for twenty years, and all of us thought he didn't have the gumption. I'll just be damned.

Thurman tried again to get himself under control. He wiped his hand hard across his mouth in a downward motion in an attempt to physically rub out the smile. It was partly successful, and for a few seconds he was able to stare at the preacher calmly, but then he had to drop his head again. I'll say this for him, he was thinking, Ol' Joe didn't go half way. That's a lot of woman. Joe had been such a mild-mannered little guy you wouldn't think he would pick a woman like that. A picture of what Joe and the lady would look like walking down the street together came into Thurman's head and the laugh began working like gas in his stomach again.

It was a long time before he could get serious. His shoes were new and his feet hurt, and that helped, but he was still unable to get his mind off the lady with the red-gold hair and the electric blue dress until his gaze fell to the drab little kid beside her. Poor kid, he thought again. What in hell is going to happen to her? Nothing good, that's for sure.

Everything got quiet all of a sudden and he realized that Reverend Arbuckle was praying and the service was at an end. He was just turning to go back to his pickup when he noticed that Bill Barstow was motioning for him to wait. He stood there while the black-suited mortician walked over to him and said in a low voice, "Thurman, I've got to make it to the bank before three o'clock and it's a quarter of now. Give me the keys to your pickup, and you drive the Buick back." Bill used the Buick instead of the Cadillac when there were no more than two or three loved ones to be taken to the cemetery. "You'll have to take the girl back to Pruitts', and I guess you'll have to do something with that woman, too. I don't know who the hell she is or where the hell she came from."

Thurman nodded his head, took his pickup keys out of his pocket and handed them over. He said, uncertainly, "Suppose I ought to take her down where the Greyhound stops?"

"Damned if I know, Thurman," Bill said, and walked off.

Thurman smoothed his suit and went over to The Kid and said, "I'll take you back." He turned to the lady and said, "And you, too, ma'am?"

The lady had her hand inside the neck of her dress, adjusting a strap. She smiled and said, "Much obliged."

Thurman motioned toward the Buick where Bill had parked it on the wrong side of the road that looped through the cemetery. The girl and the lady went toward the car and he went around them and opened the back door. The kid climbed in and scooted across the wide, soft gray seat. The lady's blue dress loomed at him as she bent to get inside, and he looked away politely. When she was all settled, she tugged the hem of her dress downward to try to cover her knees, looked back at Thurman and said, "Would you mind getting my suitcase, Mister?"

Thurman had forgotten about it. He closed the door, picked it up off the grass and put it in the trunk. He slammed the lid down, went around and got in behind the steering wheel, and laying his right arm on the back of the seat, turned and spoke to them. "I'll take you to the Pruitts," he said, his voice trailing off because he didn't know the child's name. Then, to the lady, "And where would you like to go, ma'am?"

Quickly, and without looking at the woman, The Kid said "We're goin' home."

Thurman hesitated. "Home?"

"Yes, sir. To our house." The kid looked at him solemnly.

"You mean Joe's house?"

Her big gray eyes looked right into him and she nodded

her head. "Yes, sir. To our house. Hers and mine." She motioned toward the lady who did not look the least bit surprised.

Thurman moved around in the seat and turned the key in the ignition. The Buick pulled slowly out onto the graveled road. The engine was so quiet he could hear the gravel going *sput...sput* under the tires. He thought about the two in the back and frowned. What the heck is going on, he asked himself. Then for the second time in the hour, his eyes widened as the light dawned. I get it! The woman is going to live in Joe's house with The Kid! Again he felt a kind of amazed respect for Joe Bosley. Can you believe Ol' Joe had it all worked out? Thurman shook his head as he slowed the car and automatically checked both directions before driving out on the highway. I never thought he had it in him. He had the whole thing tied up in a neat little package. Thurman tipped his head to the side and *tsked* through his teeth.

The only problem, as Thurman saw it, was that those two females had never laid eyes on each other before the funeral. He shifted his position a little so without moving his head he could watch them both in the rear view mirror. The woman was pulling some pins out of her hat. She took it off and laid it in her lap, sighing, then fluffed out that haze of red-gold hair. The Kid just sat there, not looking up.

After a while the big woman looked down at her and said, "What's your name, honey?"

Thurman watched the little girl's face lift and light up. "Amber Jean," she said, with a big wide smile, like she'd been searching for something to say the whole time. Thurman was surprised to see she wasn't as plain as he thought.

"Well," the woman said, "that's a pretty name. Mine is Nellie." Her voice was low and husky. The Kid looked like she would never take her eyes off of the woman. Like she couldn't get enough of her. Like she was afraid she would disappear like a fairy godmother.

Thurman turned his attention back to his driving and brought the Buick down to twenty as they entered the town formed by a row of houses on each side of the highway. There was silence in the back seat. At the four-way light in the middle of town, he braked gently to a stop, then pulled ahead. Two blocks farther on he flicked on his left turn signal and waited for a truck to pass, then made a U-turn across the highway and parked in front of Joe's house.

He got out and went to the trunk and got the suitcase. The Kid didn't wait for him to open the car door. She had crawled over the lady's feet and got out, and was holding the door open for the woman who slid out awkwardly, her clothes hanging up on the upholstery. Thurman set the suitcase down quickly to offer her a hand.

When she stood beside the car, a good two inches taller than Thurman, she let out a long breath and stared quietly at the house. The Kid was watching her anxiously. Then Thurman saw the lady's black eyebrows lift and her head nod in a little gesture that said she liked what she saw.

"Here," he said, "I'll take the suitcase."

"I'll get it," said the little girl, and jumped in front of Thurman and grabbed the handle with both hands.

"Honey, you can't lift that!" the lady said, bending down and making a move to push the child's hands off of it.

"I can too," the little girl said, and to prove it she got a better hold and lifted the suitcase in front of her. The effort made her grunt. "See?" she puffed, and smiled happily up to the lady.

"You'll hurt yourself," the woman said, still bent over like she would take the suitcase.

"No, I won't," the girl insisted, and began to walk, leaning far back, the suitcase slamming heavily against her legs with every short step.

"Honey..." the lady's voice started, and then stopped, as the little girl turned back with a triumphant smile. When she got to the gate she clung to the handle with one hand and opened the gate with the other, as if she were afraid the suitcase would be taken from her. The lady stepped to the side as the girl struggled through the gate, and Thurman saw her face working strangely. Her eyes misted up and her nose got red.

She looked at him. "Thank you, Mister. We'll be okay now."

There was nothing to do but leave, so Thurman walked around the Buick and opened the door. With one foot in the car he put his right arm on the roof and watched. The Kid was inching up the narrow sidewalk, the suitcase banging hard against her knees. Behind her, hovering like a hen with a new chick, her great arms bent out at the elbows, followed the lady. Under all that fat, every muscle was tensed, ready to jump and help The Kid at any second. She had one hand poised above the child's shoulder as she shuffled along behind, the toes of her sling pumps pointing out so she wouldn't step on the little girl's heels.

It took them a long time to get to the front steps. Then the lady bent down and said something and The Kid looked up at her with the same shining smile and shook her head. She started pulling and hauling and got the suitcase up on the first step then the second one. Thurman saw an expression of pain on the lady's face. He could tell she wanted to help so bad she couldn't stand it, but knew it wasn't the right thing to do.

Finally the girl, the lady, and the big suitcase were on the little porch and Thurman released his own breath as if he had been in the struggle himself.

The Kid sort of squatted behind the suitcase, and bracing her feet, shoved it across the porch. Then, her face beaming, she stood straight and felt in her pocket and brought out a key. She handed it to the woman who bent down, exposing the backs of her fat knees, and fiddled with the door. She tried the knob and it opened a crack. The Kid shook her head up and down and motioned for the lady to go in first.

Thurman watched the lady bend down and cup her huge hand under the little girl's face and lift it close to hers. She said something he couldn't hear. Then together the little girl and the woman grappled with the suitcase and wrestled it over the threshold. As the Kid turned around Thurman saw she wore a smile that nearly split her face. She closed the door behind them.

For a long time Thurman stood there on one foot, his arm resting on the top of the shining black Buick, and let the warmth of some special feeling work through him.

"Yes, ma'am," he said softly. "You're going to be okay now. You're both going to be okay now."

Then quickly he pushed the door out with his left hand and slid into the seat. Turning the key, he looked back over his shoulder to check for cars, and the Buick pulled onto the highway. He was grinning when he said aloud, "By God, Joe Bosley, you did one hell of a job. Yes, siree, Joe...one hell of a job."

# End October

Eldon Johannsen raised the axe high and brought it down in the center of the slab. With a loud, tearing crack it split into two pieces the right size for the cookstove.

He looked at the mountain of wood to be split and wondered if he could ever make himself finish it. He had been at it no more than half an hour, and already he was tired. Part of the weariness had nothing to do with the aching in his back and the hurting in his shoulder, and he knew it. Admitted it. Hell, when he was a young man he chopped wood just to finish so he could go on to some other hard job. Now, there wasn't ever anything to go on to that mattered. It was all he could do just to keep himself and Mattie alive from one day to the next, never mind seeing beyond that. Every summer he chopped the wood and when it was split and stacked in the woodshed then they would sit down and wait for winter. Nothing to look forward to except another wet spring, another hot summer with its wood to chop, another still, dry fall, and then another winter when some days were too much for the woodstove, and he and Mattie didn't ever get warm.

He bent and picked up a stick of wood and then another and threw them on the nearby pile. He didn't see or hear the boy who rode down the road, swung into the weeds that bordered the drought-yellowed yard and jumped off the bicycle. The back wheel was still spinning as the bike dropped to the ground, the spokes glinting like a Fourth of July sparkler. Eldon didn't know anyone was around until the kid spoke.

"Hi. Watcha' doin'?"

Startled, Eldon jerked upright, putting his hand to the pain in his back. He tipped his head to peer through his bifocals at the boy. Slowly he lowered the axe head to the carpet of fresh pale gold wood chips scattered on the silvered splinters of years gone by.

After a silence, he said, "What does it look like I'm doin'?"

"Choppin' wood?" the kid said with a grin. Eldon saw a black square in his mouth where he had lost a tooth. Thick red hair grew straight up from his forehead. Smart blue eyes under nearly white eyebrows were sizing Eldon up.

"Yes," Eldon said, still staring at the boy through his glasses, "as any damned fool can see, I'm choppin' wood." He moved the axe to one side, bent down and gripped a slab of bark-crusted wood and balanced it on end on the big stump that was criss-crossed with deep cuts. He swung the axe and brought it down, feeling the arthritis grab at his shoulder. The slab split and he bent over to pick up the pieces. He closed his hand around one but before he could throw it, the kid jumped in and snatched up the other piece.

"You want me to throw it on that pile?" he asked, looking up at Eldon, pale eyes squinting against the sun.

Eldon didn't answer, just tossed the wood. The kid took no answer for a 'yes,' and threw the chunk he held onto the pile. But he threw too hard and it rattled across and fell to the other side, taking several more with it.

"Huh oh," he said, and grinned easily up at Eldon as he trotted around, gathered up the fallen pieces and pitched them back on the mound.

Eldon was trying to ignore the boy. He balanced another slab on the stump and swung at it. As the crack sounded, the kid jumped in and grabbed up the two sticks of wood.

"Hey!" Eldon snapped. "What the hell do you think you're doin'? You want to get your skull split open?"

The little boy acted as though he didn't even hear. He threw the sticks onto the pile and, still grinning, looked up at Eldon. Rubbing his hands on the back of his denim pants, he said, "I can help you for awhile. My mama won't be lookin' for me."

Eldon stared at him. He didn't like kids. Never had, at least as he could remember. And, in his mind, today's kids were the worst. Never showed any respect for anybody else or anybody else's property. The ones that passed by the place were always throwing candy wrappers, cigarette packages and even beer bottles into the yard. Some boys from down the road had taken to hassling him and Mattie. Knocking at the door and then running. Throwing rocks against the woodshed. Things like that.

And then there was that time last year. Eldon wiped his forehead with his sleeve. That had convinced Eldon that kids today weren't just worthless, they were dangerous. It had been Hallowe'en night. A couple of boys had knocked on the door and when Eldon and Mattie didn't answer because they hadn't felt like they should use money to buy trick or treat candy, and because they were scared, the boys had broken it open, tearing the latch right out of the rotten old wood. They said they wanted money. They were big kids, almost grown men, and their shoulders were wide and strong where they strained at their plaid flannel shirts. One of them had a half full beer bottle dangling from one hand, and he kept saying, "Trick or treat, Old Man, trick or treat." Eldon would never forget the kid's stupid grin. He had gone weak with relief when a car came down the road and scared the kids out of the house.

For awhile after they left, he had been so afraid he couldn't move. And the worst part was knowing in his heart, for the first time, that the stupid kid was right. That he was an old man. Too old to protect himself and his wife, much less his home. Later they had talked about going to the neighbor's down the road and calling the sheriff, but they were afraid the kids would come back and hurt them if they did. It would have been useless, anyway. The sheriff never did anything to kids these days.

There was another reason, too. One he hadn't talked to Mattie about. He was humiliated, and if they'd gone to the telephone, then the neighbors would have known what happened. And they would have felt sorry for him and Mattie. Eldon couldn't stand that.

He looked at the little boy beside him out of the corner of his eye. How long before he would do something like those boys had done? Or worse. Oh, sure, he seemed like a nice boy, but nowadays you could never be sure about anyone.

All at once he felt ashamed. Hell, the kid only wanted to help. And he couldn't be more than six—not big enough to hurt anybody. And he was alone. Eldon's hand moved up to rub his shoulder. He could sure use some help.

"Well, I guess you can help for a bit," he said. "But be careful. Stay back till I tell you to come and pick it up."

The kid grinned his snaggly grin and took one step back. He spread his feet apart and planted them solidly, then put his hands behind him and clasped them together like he had seen grown-up men do.

"You live here?" he asked.

Eldon had gone back to his work. "Ummm," he grunted.

"How come you're choppin' wood?"

"For winter."

"Winter's a long time away."

"Sooner than you think."

"How come you're choppin' so much?"

"Because we need it for the stove."

"We got a gas stove."

"Can't afford gas."

"What's your name?"

"Johannsen."

"What's your other name?"

"Eldon."

"This your place?"

"Ummm."

"How come your hair's white?"

"Because I'm old, dammit."

"You got any kids?"

"No kids."

"What kind of a car have you got?"

"Don't have a car."

"How do you get to the store?"

"Walk."

"Don't stuff get heavy?"

Eldon straightened up, waving his gnarled hand around his head as if to brush away flies. "For Christ' sake, boy, don't you ever shut up?"

The boy looked startled and then dropped his head and shuffled his feet. Awkwardly he stuck his hands down deep in his pockets.

Eldon stared at him a long time, and then, as he went back to his chore, said softly, "You can help if you want to. But don't talk so much." He was sorry he had been sharp with the kid. It had been a long, long time since Eldon had been sorry about anything but his own life. He frowned, puzzled by an unfamiliar feeling of tenderness, as fragile as butterly wings, in his chest.

For the next half hour, the boy picked up the firewood and tossed it on the pile as Eldon split it. Then he shaded his eyes and looked up at the afternoon sun. Rubbing his stubby, pitch-stained little hands on his tee-shirt, he said, "I gotta go now. My mama will be lookin' for me." Then he added, bobbing his head up and down as he talked, "Don't worry, though, I'll come back tomorrow and help." He spun around and broke into a run toward the bike lying in the weeds.

Silently Eldon watched him go. He started to turn away, but couldn't. "Hey," he called, "what's your name?"

The boy skidded to a stop, jumped off the bike, dropped it to the ground, turned around and grinned. "Jimmie. Jimmie Watson. I live over there." He waved his arm toward the houses that lined both sides of the highway where it was called Main Street.

"Aren't you quite a ways from home for a little kid?"

Jimmie drew himself up as tall as he could and tucked in his chin. "Heck," he said, swaggering his weight from one foot to the other, "I come down this road a lot. My mama don't care, as long as I get home for supper."

"Well, Jimmie," Eldon said, rubbing his shoulder without knowing it, "you better get along now."

"Okay, Eldon," the boy said in that way that some kids have that lumps all people together as equals no matter their ages or colors or conditions. "See you tomorrow."

The boy grabbed the handlebars of his bicycle and jerked it up. He threw his leg across, jumped on and began to pump, standing up on the pedals and pulling up hard with his hands. When he was moving fast he gave the handlebars a quick fling and spun around, throwing gravel in an arc behind him, and yelled, "Bye, Eldon." He was smiling his snaggled grin and waving. He turned again and Eldon watched him ride off down the road, swinging the bike from side to side as he pumped. Unbidden and unwelcome, a faint memory of the small boy he was a lifetime ago stirred in his chest.

The kid was almost out of sight before Eldon shook his head and turned away. He was surprised to see how the woodpile had grown. His shoulder hurt and pain throbbed in his back. That's enough for today, he thought, and dragged himself toward the house, the pain keeping him from standing straight.

He sat on the porch beside the crooked steps and pulled off his age-hardened work shoes. With a sigh he rested his elbows on his wide-spread knees and looked at the hard, bare ground between his feet. One of the shoes dangled from his hand. *Tired. Tired.* All at once he felt like crying.

Hoarsely he muttered, "Life is a pile of shit. Too damned hard and too damned long. And it *hurts.*" Those were the words he put to his feeling, but Eldon knew they were the wrong ones. It wasn't life that was eating him, it was a little niggling fear, and the words that belonged to it were that he was afraid that ugly little red-headed kid who wouldn't stay out of the way, and wouldn't stop talking—that the kid had lied to him and wouldn't come back like he said he would.

He rubbed his hand hard across his eyes, then let his shoulders droop. Taking a deep breath, he picked up the other shoe and began to bang them both against the edge of the porch. The effort and the racket jarred the dirt and wood splinters off of his shoes and the little fear out of his head.

"Hell. I'll never see that kid again. Good riddance. The last thing kids want to do these days is work. All they want to do is make people's lives more miserable than they already are. And kids are all alike. Never try to fool yourself about that, Old Man."

Eldon got up and went inside. He walked stiffly across the linoleum and dropped his heavy shoes behind the stove. In the winter he left them there to dry, and there seemed to be no reason not to put them there in the fall. Mattie never got around to sweeping out behind the stove anyway, so what dirt he carried in wasn't going to hurt anything.

Mattie was standing at the kitchen sink, peeling potatoes with a knife, cold water running from the single faucet. She didn't look around. Neither of them spoke.

Air hissed out of the cushion as Eldon eased himself into the old Naugahyde chair. He rested his hands on the arms and rubbed his fingers idly back and forth on the soiled adhesive tape patches, then raised a hand and pinched his fingers against the bridge of his nose, pulling the thin flesh upward. He remembered, and longed for, the feeling of all's well that used to come to him at the end of the day.

Eldon gave in to his weariness, closing his eyes and putting his head back. His breathing became more regular and his mouth dropped open. He fell into a state of half-consciousness, his body sleeping and his mind aware of, but not disturbed by, the low, familiar sounds Mattie was making. Expressions played about his face and once he raised one hand in a pushing-away motion.

Like a long, slow train, hazy sun-washed scenes from his childhood rolled through his mind. In one it was early morning and he raked dew-damp hay into a pile that his father lifted with a pitch-fork into a wagon. In another he squatted with his grandfather beside the pond and the old man showed him how to make a whistle out of a hollow reed. In another he felt the hot sand under his bare feet as he ran happily down a country lane with a playmate. When he looked at his friend, he saw he had short red hair that stood up from his forehead, and pale eyes.

Mattie slid the iron skillet loudly across the stove and Eldon jerked awake. He was vaguely angry. He resented the thread of dreams that had picked at his sleep, trying to unearth feelings he had buried. Feelings that threatened to force him out of his self-exile of cynicism and hopelessness. He had spent thirty years painting himself with the shellac of bitterness, and now, in the time it took for a kid to ask, "Whatcha'doin'?" his shell was crazed with hairline cracks.

Impatient, he got to his feet and went to the window. He saw, and accepted, the ugly black scrub oaks across the road but was able to shut out the beauty of the rich copper-colored sky behind them. The kid's face, though, was there. Kept rising to the top and he couldn't push it down. It was like trying to submerge an innertube in a tub of water.

"Shit," he said, and went back to his chair.

"What?" Mattie asked, without looking at him.

"I said 'shit'." He leaned his head back again. The grease sizzled around the potatoes and the smell mixed with smells of burning wood and of bodies and clothes too long unwashed. Eldon saw the water-spotted fiberboard ceiling and closed his eyes.

Mattie ran water in the coffee pot and set it, hard, on the stove. It rattled and reminded Eldon, as she had meant it to, that they were too poor to live comfortably. That hardly anybody heated and cooked with one cookstove nowadays. She had long since stopped complaining about it. They both knew it would be cheaper to buy gas than to keep buying a load of wood every summer, but Eldon was afraid to take the little money they had put away against a time when one of them might get bad sick, to buy a gas stove and pay for having the gas piped in from the road. So Mattie sullenly cooked only what she had to to keep them alive. Whatever was cheapest and easiest. Eldon couldn't remember when she had baked anything.

He sighed again and rubbed his white hair back from his forehead and tried to think about other things. There was the kid's face again. *Go away, you little bastard!* He sat up and leaned forward and fished angrily through the outdated newspapers lying beside the chair.

"Come on," Mattie said.

Wordlessly he went to the table. On the stained oilcloth, threadbare in the middle, were the bowls of potatoes and bacon grease gravy. Canned peas were in the saucepan Mattie had warmed them in, setting on a heavy, soiled potholder. She dropped a loaf of bread still in its wrapper beside his plate. On a saucer was part of a half-melted stick of margarine. Crumbs from an earlier meal clung to it. Eldon dished out the potatoes and plopped the thick, grayish gravy on top.

Mattie pulled her chair out and sat, sighing as she lowered her weight. They didn't look at each other and for some time they ate in silence. Then Mattie, her voice flat, asked, "Who was that out at the woodpile?"

Eldon glanced up at her and she looked down at her plate and pulled a strand of stringy hair behind her ear. He didn't know she had seen the kid.

"Just some nosey kid from town." He went on chewing his food.

There was a silence as Mattie thought about whether she cared enough to go on with the conversation. She spread margarine and then jelly on a slice of bread.

"What did he want?"

"Nothing."

"Stayed a long time."

Eldon was irritated at having to talk. "Little bastard thought he was helping me."

Mattie put one elbow on the table and rested her head against her fist while with her other hand she worked the edge of her fork to cut through the hard fried crust on the potatoes. "Well, I hope he doesn't get to be a pest."

Eldon laid down his fork and let his arms hang at his sides. He ought to say that he would make damn sure the kid wouldn't be a pest. That's what he ought to say. But he didn't want to say that. He wanted to say, *'Come back, kid.'*

The blade of the axe struck the slab in the right spot, but there was a knot in the wood and it didn't split. Eldon winced as pain burned in his shoulder, but there was something satisfying about it. It brought him back to real life—where something hurts you most of the time.

For an hour he had been working, but his mind hadn't been on what he was doing. Every time he picked up another chunk of wood, he had glanced up the road toward town. He had to keep reminding himself of his motto: never expect anything good and you'll never be disappointed.

With his left hand he changed the angle of the slab and tried again. There was a crack and two pieces clattered to the ground. There. All you have to do, he thought, is pay attention to your business. He had always done his own work and he'd do it for the rest of his life. Nobody, least of all some sawed-off, red-headed kid, was going to help. With purpose he picked up the sticks and threw them onto the woodpile. Behind him there was a sound and he felt the thud of his heart in his chest.

"Hi, Eldon," the boy said.

Eldon turned and smiled. His face felt strange.

"How ya' doin', Eldon?"

"All right." He couldn't take his eyes off the little boy. "All right, I guess."

"Mama said I could go to the post office with her today, but I told her you would need me to help," Jimmie said.

Eldon was quiet for a moment, his eyes wandering, greedy, over the ugly little face. He started to say thanks, but when he spoke, the words were, "Well, I guess we better get to it."

"Where'd you get this wood, Eldon?"

"Olsen' Wood Yard."

"How'd you get it here?"

"They delivered it."

"Where'd they get it?"

"Hell, I don't know. Probably from some farmer that had to clear his land."

"What would he do that for—clear his land?"

"So he could plant a crop on it."

The boy was working hard, jumping in to pick up the split wood and then hopping back out of the way of the axe as Eldon swung. "What kind of a crop?"

"Maybe alfalfa. Or corn."

"I like corn. You like corn, Eldon?"

"Yeah. I like corn, I guess."

"Does your mama fix corn for you?"

Eldon laughed, and the sound startled him. He coughed and then said, "Well, Jimmie, I don't have a 'mama' any more. You must mean does my *wife* fix corn for me."

"Yeah. Does your wife fix corn?"

"Sometimes."

"Where is she?"

"She's in the house." Eldon's voice was sharp.

"Don't she ever come out?"

"Sometimes."

The boy was silent. For some time they worked steadily. Eldon felt good. His shoulder didn't hurt much at all. And they were getting a lot of wood split.

"Boy! It's hot, ain't it, Eldon?"

"Yes."

"I'm thirsty. Can I have a drink?"

A strange feeling swept over Eldon. He didn't want the kid in the house. *What the hell is the matter with me?* And then he knew. *Jesus Christ. I'm ashamed to have a snot-nose kid see my house and my wife. Jesus Christ.*

Grimly he said, "Okay. We'll go to the porch and have Mattie bring us some water."

"Who's Mattie?"

"My wife." Eldon buried the blade of the axe in the big

stump and left it there. The boy trotted along beside him, and when they reached the steps, Eldon called, "Mattie?"

The door with its peeling paint opened slowly and Mattie stepped out on the porch, self-consciously smoothing her stained housedress over her stomach.

"Mattie," Eldon said, "this is Jimmie. He needs a drink of water. I do, too."

Without speaking Mattie went back into the house. Eldon could hear her take one of the aluminum ice trays out of the old refrigerator. She hadn't made ice water in a long time.

Eldon let himself down onto the steps and Jimmie sat beside him. He glanced at how Eldon put his feet on the step in front of them and placed his just the same way.

"You go to school, Jimmie?"

"I'm goin' to school this fall. I'm six years old. I bet you didn't know that." He spread his hands on his knees, pulled his shoulders up around his neck and grinned up at Eldon like he'd really put one over on him. "I'm gonna be in the first grade."

Eldon looked off into the sky so the kid couldn't see he was smiling.

Mattie came out. She had a glass of ice water in each hand. She had combed her hair.

Jimmie came back the next day. And the next. Eldon and the boy worked and sweated and Eldon answered the kid's questions. Sometimes when they sat on the steps and drank their ice water, Mattie would bring out a kitchen chair and sit and listen to them. She'd have her hair combed and sometimes she would put on a clean apron.

Eldon told the kid about things he did when he was a little boy, and the kid turned his freckle-spattered face up to him, his mouth open and his eyes darting back and forth between Eldon's. The kid asked stupid questions and said funny things and hardly a day passed that Eldon and Mattie didn't have to laugh out loud about something he said or did.

One day when Eldon and the boy went to the porch for

their water, Mattie held the door open and said, "Why don't you just come on in."

Eldon wasn't even through the door when he could smell the difference. Laundry soap and Clorox and something good to eat. The whole front room had been mopped, even behind the stove, and the dishes were all done up and the cabinet top wiped clean. On the table were three glasses of ice water and a plate with cookies on it. Eldon looked at Mattie. She had washed her dress and it was starched and ironed. Her hair was smoothed back and fastened with bobby pins. When she saw him looking at her, she turned away.

"Sit down, Jimmie," she said.

"My mama makes me wash my hands before I eat."

"All right. Come over here." Mattie led him to the sink and turned on the water for him. He rinsed his hands carelessly and wiped them on a ragged towel she held out to him. Eldon watched, then shuffled over to the sink and washed his hands.

Nearly every day then, Mattie had some kind of a treat, even if sometimes it was only white bread with margarine on it, sprinkled with sugar and cinnamon. But she would cut the bread in an "X" and stack the pieces on a plate and it looked nice. When they finished, they would sit and talk and laugh awhile and then Eldon and Jimmie would go back to work.

One day Jimmie saw beans soaking in a big pot on the cabinet and asked Mattie what they were for. She told him they were going to have beans and cornbread for their dinner at noon the next day and he said he liked beans and cornbread. Eldon told him to ask his mama if he could eat with them. So the next day he came early and they ate together.

It got so he did that every few days. Then he would help Mattie with the dishes. She would get out the big old gray enameled dishpan and put soap in it and wash everything. When the dishwater was all gray and greasy from the dishes, she'd pour it down the sink and fill it up again with hot water from the teakettle on the stove and rinse them. Then Jimmie would help dry.

When Eldon would say, "Time to go back to work," sometimes Mattie would follow Jimmie to the door and put her hand out like she was going to pat his cheek or stroke his coarse hair, but she never did.

Then one day the wood was all split, and Eldon and Jimmie started loading the pieces into the wheelbarrow and pushing it into the musty half-dark woodshed to stack it in neat rows. Once Eldon said, "Get in" and Jimmie hopped into the wheelbarrow and Eldon pushed it around the yard, making it lean far over to one side and then the other. Jimmie hung on for dear life and giggled and yelled. Mattie watched from the porch and they all laughed.

Even when the wood was all stacked, Jimmie came every day. Eldon and Mattie started getting up and getting the house straightened up before he came. They would dust or mop or wash the kitchen window if it needed it. Mattie dug around in a box and found some of Eldon's shirts that she had been meaning to mend, and got them washed up and ironed so he had several changes. Eldon painted the door and braced up the steps.

Then one day when Jimmie came he was all excited. "Tomorrow my mama's gonna take me to school."

It was a quiet day. They didn't do much and they didn't talk much. When Jimmie left, Eldon sank into the old chair and Mattie went to the cabinet and began to fuss around.

After a long time she said, "I guess he won't be back."

Eldon put his head back against the Naugahyde. Presently he said, "He'll make new friends at school."

Mattie didn't look around and she didn't answer.

He sighed. "That's the way kids are nowadays. They don't give a damn about old folks."

Mattie wiped the cabinet top with the dishrag even though it didn't need it.

When she didn't say anything Eldon got up and went to the window. "Yeah. Little bastards don't care about nothing or nobody. That's the way they're brought up these days."

Mattie went over and stood where she could see past him out the window. The weeds had all gone yellow and dry. She moved to the table and sat down in the wooden chair. Eldon walked over and sat in his chair.

They were right about Jimmie not coming back.

For a time Eldon went outside every day and puttered around late in the afternoon about the time he thought school would let out. He'd look up the road toward town occasionally, but nobody ever came. So he quit going outside.

He and Mattie began to wait for winter. Eldon sat in the old chair most of the time, and re-read tattered newspapers and magazines. Or watched Mattie at the sink, fixing their supper or washing the dishes.

The days grew shorter but seemed longer, and the dust built up behind the stove. Mattie sat at the kitchen table and looked out the window. The yellowed weeds turned brown and fell to the ground. It rained and streaked the window and it was hard to see out.

The big kids came once and threw gravel on their porch and scared the hell out of them. God-damned-son-of-a-bitchin' kids! Every kid alive ought to be horse-whipped!

Winter came with the last days of October. Eldon moved the Naugahyde chair closer to the cookstove and Mattie brought the wooden chair from the table and set it on the other side. Glistening crystals of frost grew up the windows at night and then melted in the sun of the morning and ran down on the window sill and wetted the already rotting wood. Eldon smiled grimly. The frost was like everything beautiful—just something bad in pretty clothes, waiting to hurt you in some way you hadn't thought about.

Then it was the thirty-first. Halloween. Eldon woke up full of that kind of anger that comes from fear, and as the morning wore on, his anger grew. Several times he and Mattie looked at each other.

Finally, Mattie asked the question out loud. "Think we better go get some candy?"

"No, by God! This is our place and, by *God*, I'm not going to bribe a bunch of no-good stupid kids not to tear it up."

Mattie turned away. She wondered what he thought they could do to stop them.

All afternoon they sat in their chairs near the cookstove, not talking. Not even looking at each other. As the pale winter sun dropped behind the leafless scrub oaks across the road, Eldon got out of his chair and began to pace about, stopping once in a while to look out the window into the darkening sky.

It was full dark, and they were ready. Eldon swallowed at a sick anticipation. He could feel the darkness beyond the door teeming with danger and humiliation and he was brittle with dread. Mattie stood beside him and they waited. Waited. Waited. Prepared.

They were drawn wire-thin and so when the first piercing cry of the night—

*"TRICK OR TREAT!!"*

—split the silence, it was as the crack of a starter's gun, and the terror inside them burst and executed their plan without their participation. Even as he acted, Eldon knew. He heard the hoarse little voice and his heart wrenched in recognition. *No, oh, God, no.* But even knowing, he could not stop. He became a spectator to his own violence. His arms, strengthened by fear and reflex, crashed the door open to the small hobo with the red hair peeking from under a battered felt hat. He saw the pale eyes widen and he saw the boy turn aside and he saw Mattie's face crumple. The act, begun, finished of its own. The dishpan in her arms completed its arc and disgorged its stinking, greasy contents, swimming with bits of food like warm, watery vomit, over the boy.

The great pain-filled sob that shuddered through the little body became a shockwave that struck and jolted the old man and his wife. The little hobo's hat fell as he ran into the mouth of the night, and Eldon never knew whether the whimper that he heard came from the boy or from deep in his own damaged soul.

# Golden Anniversary

William and Claire Holmes sat side by side on the sofa before the white hearth with its sleek marble facing. They watched the smokeless blue flame dance about the gas logs as if looking for a place to touch down. William's left hand, and Claire's right, held crystal glasses in which champagne sparkled. His right hand rested on her left and both lay on the fine cream-colored silk of the cushion between them. Twinkling on her exposed finger was a ring set with one exquisite sapphire. The same finger found an old cigarette burn in the cushion, explored the loose threads of its frayed edges briefly and then covered it.

Claire's white hair was brushed back from her brow in a smooth wave. A single strand of perfect pearls lay at the throat of her black wool sheath. Her legs, slender and still well-formed, were angled slightly away from the center line of her body and crossed at the ankles. The fragrance of good perfume about her almost covered a faint musty odor. On her rose-tinted lips was a poignant smile, but in her eyes was a spark of excitement. Or, perhaps, anticipation.

William, too, smiled, and it was the same smile, gently sad, but also lifted with that hint of anticipation. He sipped his champagne and moved the long aristocratic fingers of his right hand on Claire's. His nails were carefully filed and buffed. He was freshly shaven and talced and the gray mustache, as thin as a pen line, was well-trimmed. The folds of his white ascot were precisely arranged inside the lapels of his smoking jacket.

Through the slit where the draperies did not quite meet came the blinking of a neon light and on the street below a raucous engine spat and tires squawled. A frown flitted on William's brow and Claire's fingers, under his, moved in a comforting way. Once the neighborhood had been quiet and elegant, the handsome new Frank Lloyd Wright building occupied by only the best people. And inside, Claire thought, as she glanced around the room, it was the same. The apartment itself retained the uncluttered, clean, tasteful look they had searched for as newlyweds.

"Have I told you, William, how much I adore the home you provided for me?"

The silence accommodated the smallest hesitation. "It is small."

"But perfect for us."

"I've loved it most because you were here, Claire."

They raised their glasses and drank.

She said, "Do you think the letter is adequate? Do you think people will understand?"

"Those who love us will."

"There are so few of them. People who love us." She paused, then added softly, "Now."

"Ah. And, so, the time is right."

A door slammed somewhere. A siren, so distant that it evoked no fear, wailed. William turned his glass in his fingers and stared into the pale liquid.

"Regrets?"

"Oh, no. No regrets." Claire's eyes scanned the loved face beside her. Then her gaze dropped to their hands on the cushion. "Oh, perhaps...if there had been children...." She glanced quickly at him, needing to be reassured one last time.

He kissed her forehead and said, "To have given me a child, Claire, might have dulled the gift of yourself. Oh, no. There are no regrets."

On the mantel the clock clicked and they both looked up, their faces suddenly somber.

They stood and touched their glasses. "To us, my dear," said William, his eyes bright with moisture.

"To us," Claire said, and her eyes, too, misted.

They took their glasses to the kitchen. Claire washed them in warm sudsy water, rinsed them, and William polished them dry, placed them on the shelf and closed the door.

"The time has come, Claire."

"Yes, William. It is time."

The plan was well and painstakingly conceived. Its flawlessness could be attributed to the calm intellectuality with which they had approached it. It had been revised and honed to perfection in the years since they had recognized the inevitable and made the decision. All effects and consequences were held up to the light of reason, one by one, and dealt with or accepted as part of the cost. The method had been researched in the most scientific manner available to them. The timing had received long and careful consideration and the date set years before. On the hall table lay the letter, precisely worded. In William's fine academic hand, it was addressed, "To Whom It May Concern."

Hand in hand they went into their bedroom. On the pillows lay the freshly laundered nightclothes they had worn on their wedding night. Though Claire had taken special care, some of the silk threads of William's dark blue pajamas had shredded at the crease marks.

They undressed, donned the nightclothes, and when they had hung the wool sheath, the smoking jacket and the pleated trousers neatly in the closet, they faced each other again.

"Now."

"Now."

"I love you more at this moment than in all the years gone by."

"And I you, William."

They went into the bathroom. On the vanity, beside the porcelain washbowl were two glasses and the small amber-colored prescription vial. In it were twenty pink pills. Ten for William. Ten for Claire. The number was critical. Fewer might not complete the process. More could make them so ill so quickly that their bodies would expel them before they could do their work.

William filled the glasses with water and handed one to Claire, placing the other on the marble vanity top. Carefully he closed the drain of the sink then picked up the prescription bottle to tap the pills into his hand.

At that moment, Claire noticed, with some distaste, that the toilet lid was not closed. She was astonished that one of them could have committed such a breach of etiquette. She intended to place her glass on the vanity, step around William and close the lid, but the glass almost slipped from her hand and, in trying to catch it, she was thrown slightly off balance and her hand struck William's elbow. Pills flew, clinking and clacking about the vanity top and rolling onto the floor.

She gasped. Though William had gone pale, he comforted her. "It's all right, my dear," he said, "I'll simply gather them up."

"Oh, my goodness, William. I am so sorry." She felt inadequate and embarrassed. It was unlike her to be clumsy and she had chosen a bad time. "I'll help you," she said, and to prove her good intentions, she picked up one of the small tablets from the vanity and dropped it into the empty vial in his hand.

"One," he said.

She found another.

"Two," he said, then retrieved two more from inside the sink.

Claire dropped to her knees, picked up a pill from the polished floor and handed it to William, trying to smile up at him. There were others scattered on the small hexagonal black and white tiles and she picked them up and handed them to William, one by one.

He dropped them into the vial, counting. Plink. "Thirteen." Plink. "Fourteen." Plink. "Fifteen."

Claire frowned and looked about her. She draped the

voluminous lace-edged skirt of her nightgown over her arm and crawled to peer into the corner of the room at each side of the door and under the kick-panel of the vanity. "Oh, William! There aren't any more!"

Though his face was drawn as he looked down at her, he tried to cover his concern. "Don't fret, my darling. We'll find them." He reached down and touched her cheek, then placed the vial on the vanity, turned and went to his hands and knees. "Don't worry, I'll find them. They must have rolled back here in the...." He crawled into the narrow space between the tub and the toilet. He had to lower his head and thrust it into the confined area, and then push his shoulders in. He strained and twisted, and as he did so, the aged silk of his pajamas gave way...*s-k-r-r-r-i-i-tt!*...and exposed a large segment of the left cheek of his buttocks. He tried to cover the rent with his hand, but he was unable to free his arms from the cramped space in which he was caught. A muffled, "Oh!" came from the place where his head was hidden.

It was Claire's turn to comfort. "Oh, darling, it doesn't matter." Dear, dear, she thought, this is not going well. Not well at all, and it's all my fault. She tried fervently not to stare at the expanse of William's pink bottom, arched upward as it was, but she was unable to take her eyes off of it. She raised her hand to her throat, feeling helpless to combat the force building inside her. The words, unsuitable, improper, unladylike, hammered at the back of her tongue and, to her horror, broke through. "My dear," she said, her voice thick with pressure, "You're blushing."

Even as shocked as she was at the ill-timed manifestation of her overdeveloped sense of the ridiculous, Claire could not get control of herself. She struggled to repress her mirth. Her shoulders shook. Tears filled her eyes. She clamped both hands tightly over her mouth. It was a tribute to the depth of her love for her husband that she was able to silence the sound. She was still staring at William's pink and naked nether region when she saw a spasm shudder through the thin body she had loved so long. His head dropped even lower under the toilet tank. Instantly she was contrite. My

God, oh, my God, she thought, I've made him cry. William, who in fifty years had not allowed himself that excess, was crying. Guilt inundated her and she sank to the floor between the vanity and the toilet, saying, over and over, "Oh, my darling, my darling, I am so sorry. Please, darling, please don't cry—William, William, William...." She squeezed herself into the opening opposite and worked her head under the tank and, when there was enough room to turn, she could see, beyond the floor flange of the toilet, his dear face. It was scarlet and wet with tears. She tried to reach him with her hand, but her arm jammed between the wall and the toilet. "Oh, my darling...." and she took a second look. He wasn't crying.

At first their laughter bubbled and squeaked and gurgled and piled up behind the toilet. Then it burst forth and guffawed and thumped off the walls. They pulled themselves out of the narrow space and sprawled, she against the vanity, he against the tub, and their laughter ricocheted off the ceiling, bounced off the mirror, swooped into the bathtub and over the shower doors. When, at last, they were too weak to laugh more, they lolled, catching their breath, going quiet, then collapsing again into laughter.

Finally they were silent. Then without speaking, they leaned forward together and peered into the bowl of the toilet. At the bottom was a small mound of pink stuff. The disintegrated and useless remains of five little pills.

They began to laugh again. It was the funniest thing they'd ever seen. They laughed until they cried.

# They Shall Have Music

My hands come to rest on the keys and I let the sounds reverberate inside me, easing the tension, erasing the weariness of happy but tiring Christmas chores. My piano. My friend. It has been my refuge since I was a very small child. Something—the twinkling of the lights on my tall and bountifully-trimmed tree, or the smell of wax from the piano, or a combination of lingering notes—evokes a long ago Christmas, and only now, almost three-quarters of a century later, do I see its true significance.

That Oklahoma night was cold and the sky, through the windows of the 1932 Ford, was the deep, intense blue that comes only on the plains in the winter. The moon, to my wonder, had traveled with us from Grandma's house, staying in exactly the same position in the frame of the window. I was amazed, but I thought such a concept was probably too advanced for my younger sister, so I stayed silent. Besides, I was too drowsy to talk. Curled up on the back seat of the car, I was warm and cozy in the burgundy and gray wool coat that my mother had made for me. My sister, in her identical coat, lay huddled against me, asleep. Part of my drowsiness was the malaise that comes to all children when the most important day of the year has past. It had been a good Christmas, with a number of gifts if you counted the handkerchiefs from aunts and the bag of treats the last day of school before the holiday, and there had been the turkey dinner and apple pie, and the running and playing and giggling and fighting with the cousins. But, it was over.

Somehow, in my lethargy and my calm consideration of the new concept about the moon, I had missed the air of excitement in the front seat where the small brown-haired woman who was our mother sat beside the trim, muscular man whom we called "Daddy." (Then, and to the end of his days. Many times I felt strange about that, and tried out the word "Dad," but it always made him seem to be someone else.) He hummed a popular tune, and smoked his Lucky Strikes, and occasionally said something that made both of them laugh.

We turned off the paved road onto the gravel, and then, soon, off the gravel onto the dirt, and I knew we were almost home.

In the row of oil field shacks beside the road, an occasional light burned, but most of our neighbors were already in bed. The little houses were of a kind—hastily tacked together to shelter the workers of Sinclair Oil Company's Plant 13 which had gone up outside the town of Seminole a few years earlier. The country was deep in The Great Depression, so men had come from everywhere for the jobs, and competed bitterly. My father was one of the lucky ones and he and Mother were happy to find the little house so close to the refinery. Like the others, it was never meant to be permanent—just something to keep out the weather until real houses could be built. But most of them remained just as they were. Ours, like the others, had never been painted, and the cutting prairie winds, the deep winter freezes and the relentless summer sun had weathered and dried it to a splintery gray. The front yards were also of a kind: hard-packed clay-like earth swept clean by diligent housewives whose degrees of worth depended upon how clean they kept their families and homes. Behind the houses were the dried remains of the drought-beaten summer gardens, old cars on blocks, and piles of used lumber and junk. Each house had its outdoor toilet.

When the car slowed, I sighed, glad to be home. We bumped across the ditch and into our yard, stopping only a few feet from the front steps, and when the engine was off, I could hear the familiar clack-boom, clack-boom of the nearby pumps that drew the stinking black crude out of the earth. Each night I went to sleep making songs to the rhythm they produced.

When Mother opened the car door, the cold and the smell of the oil fields rushed in. She said, "Come on, now." We struggled sleepily out of the car and stood shivering behind Daddy as he fumbled with the key in the lock, then went inside and waved his arm about in the darkness until he found the string from the light bulb that hung in the middle of the room.

The little house was flooded with weak yellow light. It shone on the gray, bare wood floor, the yellowed and water-spotted wall paper and the couch that Mother had covered with a well-washed cotton "Indian blanket" when the upholstery got too dirty and worn. And the light revealed a couple of straight wooden chairs and a rocker. Beside the rocker was a sewing stand and beside the couch was a smoking stand, both built with simple hand tools by my father. At the one small window there was a skimpy lace curtain that hung crooked because Mother had had to wash it after one of the dust storms, and it stretched askew when she ironed it. I remember no pictures on the wall, but there was a radio to which they listened, morning, noon and night, absorbing everything they could hear. Through a door was the one small bedroom, and in an alcove off the front room (we never said "living room" ) was the double bed in which my sister and I slept. I suppose that alcove was intended to be a dining room of sorts, since it was between the front room and the kitchen, but I loved sleeping there, going to sleep each night in the light from the front room, to the sounds of the radio, and with the warm safe feeling that came from having my parents only a few feet away.

But on that Christmas night, the yellowish light from the bare bulb that shone on all the familiar things, also fell on something new. Something astonishing! A piano! A shining, brand new piano. I had never been inside a house with a piano. It was puzzling, almost frightening, to have a thing so unusual in our front room. Mother and Daddy stared at us and Daddy kept chuckling. He said, "Well! What in the world is that?" And Mother, using our two names together as if we were one person, as she always did, said, "What do you have to say, Margie-Vangie?"

I had nothing to say. What I saw before me was beyond my scope of experience, and almost beyond the limits of my imagination. I didn't know what was expected of me. I stood quite still, holding tightly to my sister's hand, embarrassed at the enormity of the moment.

"Don't you want to open it?" Daddy said, and, with his stubby, scarred, working-man's hands, folded back the keyboard cover, very carefully as if he were afraid he might break it. The gleaming white and black keys that marched the length of the keyboard were revealed. I was stunned. There were hundreds and hundreds of them. How could anyone ever find the right ones? I knew it was possible for I had heard the church piano player.

"Come on," Daddy said, "play it."

I took one step backward. "I don't know how."

"Well, here's how." With his index finger he reached out and struck a key. It was much louder than I expected it to be. I glanced at him and smiled a little, abashed at what he had done. I wanted to just go to bed, and have a little time to get used to the strange new thing, but I knew he wanted me to go over there and touch those keys and make a sound. Still hanging onto my sister' s hand, I edged closer and then, finally, reluctantly, I reached out and pressed a key. At the clear, bell-like sound, I jerked my hand back as if I'd been burned, and Daddy laughed.

Mother, always the pragmatic one, ready to get on with things, said, "Well, do you like it?"

"Uh huh," I said. I looked at my sister. Her black-brown

eyes were enormous. "See?" I said to her. "See? It' s a piano."

She nodded her head. Being the younger, she was not required to speak.

Later, after I had taken off my coat and Daddy had lit the open-face gas heater with a wooden match, I came back and stood before the piano for a long time. When Mother said, "Come over here by the stove and I'll help you get your pajamas on," I did what she said. But I didn't stop looking at the huge new thing that had come into my life. There didn't seem to be anything else in the house. Even after I was in bed, I could see the piano in the front room and in some distant corner of my child's mind, I knew it was a thing of great importance.

I was right. From that time on, we were different. From our neighbors, and our relatives. My position in school changed. There were two or three other children in my room in the country school who took piano lessons, but they lived in the neat white-painted company houses with bathrooms and well-trimmed lawns and their fathers were the bosses. When I began to take piano lessons I was elevated slightly above the majority of the other children in the third grade. Not to the level of the children who lived in the white houses, but to some in-between place. Or, more accurately, to some spot slightly to the side. If I had a sense, then, that I had been subtly separated from the others, I never thought it in words.

I did well at my piano lessons, and advanced to a point beyond that of the others who "took." Of course, I didn't know that skill alone could never quite make a worker's child totally acceptable to the children who lived in white houses, except when the skill was useful to them, and then only on a temporary basis. So, I went from day to day contentedly unaware that I didn't quite fit anywhere, and strangely enough, I think I eventually came to like it that way. The piano had an immense effect on my life.

But it isn't just what that Christmas in the early 1930s means to me that I think of now, so many years and so many miles away from that time and place. I think of that young couple who made the daring decision to buy a piano for their little girls. It set them apart, too, and they surely must have known the risks they were taking. Paying for it would use up an inordinate share of his monthly check. They must have been aware that their very own families, their parents and their many brothers and sisters, not to mention the neighbors and the people at church and my father' s co-workers would think they were crazy. "W'y, she could have had one of them electric ice boxes for that kind of money." "Times are hard. A man's a fool to throw money away on things such as that." And even if they sensed that part of the derision was only a kind of secret envy, they must have felt like outsiders in their own little world.

Can you imagine what mental preparation it must have taken for them to make that trip to town to buy a piano? How carefully they must have dressed? And can't you see them smooth their hair before they went inside the store? How alien they must have felt to move among the grandeur of gleaming new pianos and be approached by some slick salesman in a suit. How difficult to ask, "How much?" And how uneasy they must have been as they signed their names to a legal contract that said they would pay for it "on time."

And that wasn't the end of it. Later they would have to knock on the door of a nice home in the good part of town to ask about lessons for two little girls. They would have to sit in a room with carpets and fine furniture, where their plain clothes would suddenly seem shabby. They would have to converse with an educated, refined person who would be able to see at a glance that they were not. But they did it. They did something quite daring, and so they, too, moved slightly up and out of the comfort of their familiar world.

The piano I play is a different one. My parents have been gone a long time now. But what they did that long ago Christmas had an influence not just on the lives of the young couple and their little girls and the boy who came later, but also on their grandchildren, and now their great grandchildren. Each generation has had its music. But, more important, inside each child of a child of a child, is the potential to dare to try something just a little out of the ordinary. To take that frightening step slightly to the side. It is a priceless legacy.

# Zachary's Miracle Cure

Zachary Henderson's filthy Nikes dragged in the gravel as he walked. He was tired. He was hungry. He was hot. His head itched and his armpits itched and his ass itched and his hair, hanging down the back of his neck, felt stringy and greasy. With black-lined nails he scratched his face under the month-long growth of beard. He could smell himself and was pretty sure any other person who came within twenty feet of him could, too. He was big into hate that day and of all the hate that worked inside of him, the hate for himself was greatest.

Not for the first time in his ten-month odyssey, he was down and this time he just no longer cared. About anything. He wondered what would happen if he took a little sidestep onto the pavement when he was meeting a semi. Wouldn't take much. The blacktop was narrow. The big rigs nearly touched the yellow line on one side, the white on the other. If he timed it just right... one step and...Splat! He'd be out of his misery and the world would be free of one more disgusting fuckup.

He swallowed and let out a slow, heavy sigh. "Screw it," he muttered. He didn't even have the energy to plan his own demise. One step after another. One stinking sweating foot after the other.

The late-May sun baked him through his dirty long-sleeved shirt and he thought again how good it would feel to take the shirt off. But Zachary Henderson was too smart to risk skin cancer for a fleeting moment of relief. He snorted. Smart? Aloud he muttered, "If you're so damned smart, Zach, what in hell are you doing out here for the exclusive reason of stinkin' up the countryside?" He shifted his backpack and dragged himself forward.

He hardly ever came to this: this depression about being alone, on the road, broke and hungry, but today he was lonelier, hungrier and miserably uncomfortable. This was the worst. A lot worse than he ever anticipated. He hadn't talked to anybody since the snotty assistant manager at a Dairy Queen yesterday morning said he could pick up trash and hose down the lot for a burger and fries. He'd had to negotiate for a big Coke. He hadn't eaten since then. For the ten months he'd been on the road, he'd usually managed to work for enough food to keep him going. A couple of times he'd watched people at a rest stop wrap up a perfectly good sandwich that some fat ten-year-old had taken one bite out of, and toss it in the garbage. When they'd driven off in their dirty van, he could get that sandwich. Americans would throw away their heads if they didn't have an immediate need for them, he thought. But there hadn't been any ugly American families that day or even any rest areas because he'd angled off on a rural highway.

So he was hungry and hot and stinking, depressed beyond words. When he had made the decision to hit the road for a few months, let the national recession run its course and the hi-tech companies get going again so he could land a good-paying job, he'd known there would be days like this. And he'd reasoned that he could just wait them out and the next day would be better. So far he'd managed with that bit of self-hypnosis: one hour, one day at a time. "Tomorrow's going to be easier," he'd tell himself. But this was the fourth or fifth bad day in a row and today he wasn't so sure about tomorrow. The hunger, maybe. And sleeping on the ground had lost its charm. He guessed that he'd better try to find something a little more permanent to do in the next town. Just for a few days.

He'd developed a knack of walking without knowing it. His feet did their walking while his mind went elsewhere. That's why he almost walked straight into a sign. WARNING: HITCHHIKERS MAY BE ESCAPED CONVICTS. Shit. Nobody was gonna offer him a ride. People out here in the Bible Belt were self-righteous and hard-assed. He recalled that he'd walked into a roadside park one day, past an overweight family at a picnic table, his eyes frozen on their food, his mouth watering. A woman, wearing an oversized sweatshirt and cotton knit pants stretched far beyond their intended capacity, had muttered as she made baloney and mayonnaise sandwiches for a brood of kids, "Don't look at me, boy. They's pleny of jobs out there."

There was a dead bird in his path. He had to take a sidestep to avoid it and the effort to do so was enormous. He started to kick it out of the way, but then something stopped him and suddenly he was choking back tears. Making a wet noise, he sucked in his breath and chided himself, "Oh, no. None of that sentimental crap, Zach. Just keep walking. Left foot, right foot, left foot...." His voice faded away.

Zach was a loner. A bright, intelligent, educated loner. He'd done his time in the manicured silicon valley, made lots of money, moved on and made more money and, like his co-workers, when the storm came and washed thousands of people out of the silicon valley and thousands of bucks out of their bank accounts, he worked for months trying to find another spot where he could make lots of money. Then one day he'd asked himself why. Why in hell should he put himself through all that shit just to make more money? He was twenty-six, single, owed nobody and needed nothing. The only thing he could think of that he wanted was a little solitude, and once the thought that he could simply walk away and be alone found a purchase in his mind, he did just that. Notified his landlord, sold his Porsche to the guy down the street who still had his job, paid the bank, gave his clothes, his PC, his CDs and DVDs away, and set the rest of his stuff on the sidewalk with a sign that said "FREE." The next morning he put on the new Nikes, old Levi's and a sweatshirt, crammed another pair of Levi's and some jockey shorts and socks along with an oversized waterproof poncho and a skinny sleeping bag into a pack and walked down the street. He didn't even take a map. Just started walking in a general easterly direction.

That was ten months ago. He'd survived the winter by veering south as far as I-10 and then wandering off and on and around that freeway. What he'd found out was that it could be damned cold in Southern California and Southern Arizona but if you used your head, you wouldn't freeze. Now it was late spring, hot as hell, and the thought of that cold desert rain with its jolts of lightning was pleasant. He'd begun to angle north and was well into Oklahoma when he discovered just how hot the sun could get and how little protection there was along the secondary highways. Trees, but they were little and surrounded by knee-high weeds dried hard and sharp. No little green grottos where a guy could lounge in comfort.

He knew that he wasn't much in the looks department anymore. He'd tanned to a deep sepia color and some days, when the sun was particularly searing, his face and hands turned maroon. His long-sleeved tee shirt, once white, was shades of gray, brown and pee-yellow. The Levi's, he knew, would fall apart when he put them in a laundro-mat in the next little town he came to. That is, if he were lucky enough to come across the necessary coins. Mentally he dug down deep into his backpack but there were no more Levi's. Maybe a pair of jockey shorts and maybe a pair of clean socks. He had thought about changing but his ass and his feet were so dirty he hadn't bothered.

He looked up at a graveled turn-off. On a gate made out of welded two-inch pipe was a sign. HELP WANTED. He stopped and stood staring at the sign, rubbing his back. Zach wasn't afraid of work. His dad believed kids ought to work and he'd done his share of mowing grass and painting the house and staying out at his grandpa's farm for weeks at a time to help with the haying. In college he'd worked summers on a highway crew. But he wasn't sure he wanted to deal with some ignorant farmer just for a place to sleep and some potatoes and gravy.

He pondered the question as he stared down the graveled road. He was aware that a semi was approaching but he didn't expect the driver to sound the air horn, and when he did the shock went through his weak body. "Goddammit," he muttered, and found himself walking through the gate and down the road without actually having made the decision to do so.

The road made a gentle bend and over the weeds he saw a house and a barn and a couple of sheds. A ten-year-old Taurus was parked at an angle near the back door of the house. The barn door was open and there was a new-looking John Deere tractor inside.

Zach approached the back door of the house. He knocked on the screen door, noticing that the white paint was peeling off, flakes falling onto the porch floor. He was still a bit undecided about whether he wanted to take a couple of days' work, or just lie down somewhere and die. When nobody answered, he more or less decided on the latter. He turned around and was down the steps when he heard the door open. He turned on his best smile. Even if it was false and forced, it was a good smile, helped along by the thousands his folks had paid the orthodontist, and he'd made it work for him in many situations.

"Hello," he said. "There's a sign on the gate...?" He waited. The man behind the screen door was small and wiry. He took his time sizing Zach up. His Levi's had been ironed and his white tee shirt was worn but bleached to pristine white. He had a toothpick in his mouth and slowly he put a hand up and moved it from one side of his mouth to the other. Then he said, "I guess you can't be too choosy these days." He turned and raised his voice when he spoke back into the house. "I'm going out to the barn, Billie Jean." He came out and let the screen door slam softly.

The guy was six inches shorter than Zach but still he

nearly pushed him off the steps as he came down. Zach opened his mouth to say something but caught himself in time. Silently he reminded himself, *You're hot and tired, and hungry. Just keep your big mouth shut.* He followed the silent farmer to the barn.

As they walked along the shady side of the structure, the man said, "I'm gonna need some help with the fences. Figure there's four or five days work if you're a good worker." As an afterthought he said, "Not much chance of that."

Good, thought Zach. Four or five days work would set him up for quite a while. "What do you pay?" he asked.

The farmer stopped, looked at Zach and set his jaw before he said, "That's the way it is nowadays, isn't it? Every dirty bum on the road wants union wages." He paused. Zach was silent. The farmer turned and walked on ahead, saying, "I pay a few bucks an hour, and you get food and a bed. Billie Jean's a good cook. She fixes the hired hands a plate of the same food we eat and I'll bring it out to you in the evening. Come to the back door in the morning. Coffee and biscuits. And she'll make you a sandwich so you won't have to quit workin' to come in at noontime."

For no good reason, Zach felt angry. The deal was fair but he felt like a five-year-old kid being told just how it was going to be, take it or leave it. He almost said, "Fuck it," but he bit it back. "Can I have supper tonight?"

The farmer glanced at him and said, "I guess so. I'll have to take a couple of dollars out of your pay." He led Zach past the end of the barn. Just around the corner was a door. He motioned toward it. "Cot's in there. But don't touch it till you're clean. Don't put those nasty clothes on it, either. Throw them on the floor. I'll bring out a plastic bag later tonight and I'll throw them in the washer myself. Don't want Billie Jean to have to mess with that stuff."

He led Zach to a hydrant rigged up under a small tank that apparently held rain water. "You're gonna have to have some soap to handle that kind of filth. Over there on the lumber stack. And there's a towel hanging on that nail tacked into the end of one of the two by sixes." He pointed. "You stink, boy."

Zach had to suppress the urge to hit the cocky little bastard but he knew he was right.

"I don't want you even sittin' on that cot, not till you're clean. Billy Jean keeps that bed as clean as the ones in the house. I'll bring you out something to eat pretty soon." Then he turned and walked away.

Zach watched the farmer disappear. He sighed and went through the door and into the barn. In the corner was the cot, the evening sun casting gold stripes across it through the cracks. Zach's heart jumped. He walked closer to it. Sure enough, a real bed with sheets, a pillow with a pillow case. It was the pillow case with purple pansies embroidered on it...and it had been ironed, for God's sake...that evoked the sudden and crisp image of home that almost brought him to his knees. He swallowed back a picture of his mom's face when she would come to the back door to call him and his brother in to wash up for supper.

He stood, eyes closed, for a long moment, then worked the pack off his back and dropped it beside the cot. Unbidden and unwanted, the thoughts came. He'd been a regular American kid, taken good care of along with his brother, by a mom and dad who loved them. They'd been proud when he was successful in hi-tech, and disappointed when he took to the road. But after they'd quietly reminded him of the various dangers and the damage he might do to his future, they'd shut up. They'd always done that: pointed out what an inexperienced and overconfident kid ought to look out for in life, and then they'd let him make his own mistakes. And now, in a barn in rural Oklahoma, stinking dirty, feeling keenly and miserably alone, he was crying because he missed his family and he'd made some real stupid mistakes.

He stood for a time with his hands over his face, rubbing his tears around in the dirt from the road. Up until this minute, he'd known that he could change everything, that he could head for the nearest city and land a job. Up until this minute he'd been a goddamned stupid ass. "You talk about your burned bridges," he muttered. "I've burned all my goddamned bridges, the ones behind me and the ones in front." He saw his mom's face and he remembered that when he was little and hurt himself, he would stand beside her chair and bury his face in her lap and feel her plump arms around him. He wanted his mom. But all the bridges between this fucking farm and his mom were gone. Burned.

He gave in to grief. He grieved for the good life he'd walked out on. And for his carefree childhood. For the disappointment he'd become to his mom and dad. And he mourned his own good sense. He'd left that, too, on the other side of the black, smoking ruins of the bridges.

He lifted his head and looked around him. Not even a way to put an end to himself and his misery. Barely able to move, he began taking off his clothes. When he pulled his shirt over his head he winced from the smell of it. He was still crying, and now it was because he'd violated the ordinary everyday rules of cleanliness and self pride that his folks had taught him. He smeared snot over his face with the back of his dirty hand and took off his Levi's. And then his ruined jockeys that had fit his hind end like second skin when he started out on this stupid journey. Now he couldn't remember what color they were supposed to be and the butt with a hole in it hung loose and baggy. Not that it mattered, he thought. The ass certain girls had once thought was good-looking was no ass at all anymore.

He tossed the smelly clothes onto the swept plank floor. Naked, he searched through his backpack and found a wadded but unworn pair of jockey shorts. But no more socks. He should have brought no shorts and fifty pairs of socks, he told himself. Just one more dumb mistake. With the clean shorts in his hand, he walked out of the barn and through the ankle-high grass to the hydrant. There was a hose connected to it. He stared down at the nozzle and for a moment thought he didn't have the strength to bend down, pick it up, and get up again. It took a physical and mental effort to accomplish the feat.

He was still sniffling when he turned on the water. Midsummer had warmed the earth and the earth had warmed the water so it gurgled out of the hose in a body-temperature stream. He was lifting the nozzle to douse his head when he remembered the farmer said there was soap. He hadn't seen soap for months except that stinking pink stuff in gas station rest rooms or rest areas. There, on the three-foot-high stack of old lumber was a slightly used bar of soap, the word "Camay" still readable. Just like his mom used to have in the bathroom. He picked it up. It was hard. Even when he ran water over it, it was like enamel. He worked it awhile. After a time he could see a bubble here and there.

He felt a little grin emerge. He muttered, "All right!" He raised the hose and let it run over his head. At first it just rolled off of his oily hair. Then he started rubbing the bar of soap over his head. It still didn't make foam, so he rinsed his hair and started again. That time the bubbles foamed up thick and luxurious. He rubbed and swished and massaged his head, the creamy stuff running down through his beard. He worked it with his hands, then held them up and saw that even his nails were clean. He let the water run free over his head and face until the soap was gone and his hair felt cleaner than it had ever felt in his whole life. He took in a breath and to his surprise, an involuntary sob slubbed in his throat, like when he was a kid and had been crying a long time but was getting over whatever the hurt was. That's what he was feeling, like he was getting over a hurt.

He looked around for a rag. A piece of an old flannel shirt was lying on the end of the lumber pile where somebody had spread it to dry. He wet it and made suds, laid the soap on the framework of the water tank and washed his face. He got soap in his eyes and it felt great. He laughed and quickly looked around, not sure he himself had made that sound. He stuck his fingers in all the crevices in his ears and worked them around. Foam stained tan with dirt ran down his body like dirty whipped cream. He swished the soapy rag over his neck, and his arms and his chest, the dark hair swirling and matting in the soap. His armpits got a violent scrubbing.

He hung the rag over the faucet handle and with the hose in his left hand, he half-squatted and began to wash his groin. He rubbed the bar of soap in his pubic hair and made thick rich suds. He pulled back the foreskin and washed, then swished the soap around and around his testicles, then on back to his butt, the stream of tepid water from the hose following the action, washing away the filth and soap. He sudsed up the hair on his legs and he washed away the smell on his feet that had been so bad he could almost see it. He got the rag and pulled it through all eight toe slots. And again, something he didn't expect or understand made him laugh aloud. "Once more with feeling," he laughed again, and ran the water over his head and over each wet and shining body part.

Finally the body of Zachary Henderson was clean. He high-stepped across the grass, careful to keep his feet clean, and lifted the towel off the nail. It was old, worn thin, and made rough and hard by the sun. It felt wonderful. He took great care with drying his body, ruffling his hair, being sure his ears were dry inside, raising his arms high to flick the towel in his armpits, and repeating the half-squat to dry his butt. The sun was setting, and with it the breeze riffled the grass and his hair and made him cool. He lifted his elbows outward and spread his legs and felt the wind in his armpits and in his crotch. There was unexpected joy in the ritual. He was purified.

Smiling, he went back to the hydrant and coiled the hose around the tap, trying to remember where he'd heard that the first sign that a sick animal was getting well was that it began to groom itself. He wondered, had he been sick? Actually sick? He hadn't been running a fever or puking, but there were other kinds of sick. His brows came together and he decided he had been sick. But now it hardly seemed to matter.

Now he was happy. "Happy," he murmured. Happiness was a feeling he'd forgotten about. He raised his arms, stretched, and was conscious of every square inch of the surface of his body, and every square inch felt good. He pulled on the shorts and had just climbed onto the lumber pile to sit spraddled out in the setting sun to let his hair and all his crevices dry, when the farmer came around the corner of the barn with a plate, a tea towel draped over it.

"Here," he said. "Eat it before it gets cold." He handed the plate to Zach and out of his pocket took a little packet, a spoon, a knife and a fork wrapped in a pale green paper napkin. Zach took the plate and the packet and smiled at the farmer.

The farmer stared at him then relaxed. "Well, I guess there was a human under that dirt, after all." He even grinned a bit. Then he walked away, saying, "We gotta be out at those fences before sunrise."

Zach said, "Yes, sir," and there was no sarcasm in his tone.

He watched the farmer disappear around the corner before he lifted the towel off the plate and put it aside. There was a pork chop the size of his Little League catcher's mitt, along with a big heap of mashed potatoes and gravy, a fresh sliced tomato, some green beans, a biscuit with butter running out the sides, and wrapped in another paper napkin, a square of cake with coconut icing. Zach stared, holding himself back from hogging down the food and choking himself. He scooted back on the lumber stack and folded his legs so he could place the plate in front of him. He picked up the biscuit in his left hand and the fork in his right and buried the fork deep into the mashed potatoes. Then he stopped, overcome by some emotion that rendered him unable to move.

For a long, still moment he didn't breathe, then, he gasped and came back to the present. He closed his eyes and raised his face to the heavens, stretched his arms upward in thanks to, and worship of, the patient and undefined God that was his. Mashed potatoes stained with gravy made a small gooey flag on his fork, and butter ran down his other arm from the biscuit.

His love for the world and everything in it had no bounds.

He felt lighted from the inside. He sat like a skinny Buddha, huge and omnipotent.

He threw his head back and filled his lungs with sweet evening air. Then, his voice hoarse, but solid and loud, he croaked, "I am Zachary Henderson. Zachary the Great, the Fine. Zachary Henderson, Emperor of the Universe."

And Emperor Zachary ate his supper.

# The Recidivist

At the question, unexpected outrage jolts me. I flinch and nearly cry out. That it was there, lurking inside me like an abscess, waiting for this moment to burst and shoot its heat through me, I did not even suspect. It is obscene and unwelcome. I close my ears, but I hear it. *Wait!* it hisses. *Wait! Not yet! After this moment,* it whispers, *there is no escape.* And the pain of its truth slashes me.

No escape. I have been trapped into this gross capitulation and it is not my fault. The trap closed on me when I was only a jelly-mass of fetus in my mother's womb, and locked when my own cried out for pleasure. I feel the cellular structure of my body and I hate it. The softness of my narrow shoulders and the incurving of my waist, and the hips and pelvis that give safe harbor to the traitorous womb.

Beside me is its issue. The small girl and the smaller boy, standing awkward and dependent, the boy bunching his trousers in his hand, the girl silent, resentful. I have hate for them, too, for what they have taken from me. It shocks me. Terrifies me.

And that is hardly the end of it. There is hate for two men. The one who so inconsiderately died, leaving me defenseless against, and needy of, this socially acceptable surrender, and for the one who stands beside me. Especially for the one beside me. He knew. He knew that even I, wise from being there before...even I, with my covert knowledge of I-becoming-we-becoming-he, had no choices. Did he smile as he planned the asking, knowing, as he did, that he need only tender the offer? That the offer made the decision.

Ah, but is my hate not for the boy and the girl, nor for the dead man or the living one, but for my own lack of courage? For the whining suspicion that I haven't got quite the right stuff to meet the challenge? No! Not fair! Why should it be *my* challenge? Who made these rules? Who said, with ultimate arrogance, that this is how it is? That my heart and my brain and my soul have no say in the matter of my life?

I gasp for breath. My blood pounds in my throat with such power that it tickles and I need to cough. Something is expected of me...what is it?

Oh, yes. I feel the cooling of the scalding emotions. Now I am inundated by shame for what I have allowed. I have let my mind enter forbidden territory, to savor the sweet hot taste of outrage...anger...hate. I am a miserable, ungrateful creature. I must put it all away. Forget it. There. There. Remember, this is now. Things are different now. Everything will be fine. Comfortable. Easy. It will. I will make sure it will.

A breeze from the open window moves the chiffon of my dress and cools my hot skin. My held breath is released. The flowers in my hand cease their trembling. I am calm. The face of the man beside me comes into focus, blurs once, and then is clear. In his eyes is a puzzled, expectant urgency. My hesitation—that long pause—has embarrassed him. I am sorry. How childish of me to lose control. How silly. I won't let it happen again. I smile and see relief on his face.

"I do," I say.

I hear my own voice. It is sweet and loving. Soft. Grateful. Compliant.

# The Giver

Helen stared at the open door to the examination room where they'd taken her cat. The chairs in the waiting room were arranged so you couldn't see in where they examined the animals. She guessed that was so the doctor could have the young girl who was at the front desk come and help him in there, and they could still hear if anyone else came in.

Helen's hands were cold. She was cold all over. There was something different about the cold in doctor's offices. It wasn't how cold it was as much as it was how far inside a person it went. She pulled her shoulders forward and adjusted her hairpin-lace sweater.

All doctor's offices were the same, Helen thought, whether they were people doctors or animal doctors. Didn't make any difference. A fragment of memory winged her mind: long ago someone (her grandpa?) had called dragonflies "snake doctors". Snake doctors, baby doctors, cat doctors. Doctors, sickness, pain.

The veterinarian came through the door toward her. She started, and decided, too late, not to stand. She sat perched on the front edge of the plastic seat.

"I'm afraid I'm going to have to do a couple of tests, Mrs. Wylie. It will take an hour or so. Why don't you go on home and I'll give you a call."

"No." Her voice was too loud. She softened it. "I'll just wait."

The doctor hesitated. He wore thick glasses that made his eyes look funny. Like she was looking through little round windows at eyes glued on the wall across the room. "Well, all right," he said, "if you want to. It's going to take a little while."

"That's all right," she said, and slid back on the chair. He didn't want her sitting around there, she could see that. But she wouldn't feel right about going on home before she knew what was the matter with her cat.

And it would be a lot of trouble. She'd have to let Mrs. Arkin go home, and then get her to come back over when the girl called her to come and pick up her cat. It would probably be just a few minutes, anyway.

Besides.

Helen drew her breath in and let it out. Well? She didn't have to be ashamed of enjoying a few minutes away. She hadn't had an hour of relief for a month. Not since her sister came that Sunday and made her go for a walk. She'd just as soon have stayed. It seemed impolite when Mamie could only come once in a while.

And it wasn't relief she wanted, for goodness sake. No decent person would want relief from taking care of her own mother. Why, Helen wouldn't let herself complain, not if she lost another twenty pounds. After all, it was her *mother.*

So quickly that she didn't have a chance to deflect them, words formed in Helen's mind. *That thing is not your mother!* Helen winced and turned away but it was like something had cracked open. Everything poured in on her and she smelled the sickroom and saw the ugliness and felt the pain that had turned her mother into that thing. Into nothing human. Nothing that Helen had ever known. A breathing, waxy skeleton that whined and moaned and said hard, hurtful things. A thing that would never be better. Only worse, the doctors said. Only a matter of time, they said. Only a matter of time until the pain that her mother had become would eat through another organ and the blood would pour out again and they wouldn't be able to stick enough needles or enough tubes into the thing to keep it suffering.

Outside a car horn beeped. Helen jumped and put her hands to her throat. Her heart was pounding. She swallowed something acidy that had risen into her mouth. What vile thing had come over her?

She shook her head to clear it and looked up to see the girl coming out of the examination room carrying her cat. Helen stood to go to them, but the girl just smiled efficiently and took her cat down a hall that Helen couldn't see into. She tried to imagine what kind of a place they would put her in. A cage, she supposed, and hoped there would be something soft underneath her.

She twisted on her chair and rubbed the arthritis knob on her thumb with the fingers of her other hand. The girl should have at least let her touch her cat. Stroke her once, just so she'd know that Helen was there. Of course, it was just a cat. Still.... Oh, Helen knew you ought not to let yourself get too attached to an animal. But her cat was about the only friend she had left. Her other friends had stopped coming by quite a while back. They'd been good about it at first, but after a while it was just too unpleasant. Helen was glad in a way. She didn't have to worry anymore that somebody would drop in when the whole house smelled that way.

She was happy just to have her cat. She never had to explain anything to her cat. Back when Helen still cried, her cat would let her cry into her soft gray fur as long as she wanted to, and wouldn't try to stop her like people did. Helen pursed her mouth and looked up at the ceiling and remembered how it felt when her cat wound in and out around her tired feet as she stood folding the ugly gowns and the stained sheets and rags. And just this morning, when Helen had grabbed a cracker out of the box and sank down in her rocker for a minute, why, right up there came her cat, trying to snatch a bite. Helen's mouth softened. The cat didn't even like crackers. It was just a game they played.

There was a clock on the wall. It had been forty-five minutes. The doctor would be telling her something pretty soon.

She hoped Mrs. Arkin wasn't getting too impatient. She hoped her mother would ask for the bedpan if she needed it. But she didn't ask much anymore.

She was thinking how quiet it was in the room when all of a sudden her fear for her cat escaped the place where she had put it. She prayed, "Oh, God. Oh, God, please." Was it all right with God if you prayed for a cat? She swallowed, then told herself she didn't need to be afraid, anyway. It was only some little thing. Something minor. In a few minutes she'd just write a check and smile at the doctor and the girl and take her cat home.

But she didn't. Helen knew when the doctor came out of the room. Before he even said anything, she wanted to shout out, *that's a lie!*

"I can relieve her for a time, Mrs. Wylie." He was just going ahead talking like it was something ordinary he was saying. "I'll go ahead and perform the little operation. In itself it's not dangerous, but it's painful and you need to know that some cats don't do well with the anesthesia. Some cats die from shock. I don't think your cat will, though." She watched his eyes and they measured her own and he stopped talking for a moment. "You can come and get her tomorrow if you want to. She'll be just fine for a week or so, then the fluid will begin to build up. You'll know when her pain gets too bad. Just bring her back in then; we'll draw the fluid off again. She's a strong cat. We can keep her alive for three or four months."

Helen's heart seemed enlarged. All the air had left her lungs. Her throat was constricted and her voice was hoarse and flat. "She's going to die? Something is hurting her?"

"Well, yes. There isn't any cure, Mrs. Wylie, but we can relieve her temporarily...."

Someone was screaming in the waiting room and Helen felt something raspy in her own throat. *"Take her! Now! Put her to sleep! What kind of a doctor are you? Help her die. Now! Now!"* Fists with skin stretched tight over white arthritic knuckles were pounding on the doctor's chest. Red waves washed over Helen's eyes and she was dizzy.

"Mrs. Wylie! My goodness! I just thought...."

Helen was shocked to see that the girl in the white uniform was holding her wrists. Her fingers were hard and it hurt.

The girl said, "Mrs. Wylie. It's not the doctor's fault that your cat is sick."

Helen shook her hands loose and wailed, "Then whose is it?" The sound keened around and around the room before it died. The silence was cold. The clock ticked.

"Here, Mrs. Wylie." The girl had gone to get a plastic cup of water. "Drink this."

"No." Helen shook her head. "I'm all right." She wiped her face with a tissue the girl handed her. "Just do as I say." She pulled her sweater around her thin shoulders and fumbled in her purse for her checkbook.

"Just do as I say," she whispered.

# A Time Too Soon

Maurice Cabot closed the screen door on the deep back veranda and walked, unhurried but with purpose, across the once-manicured grounds of Shadow Oaks to the old carriage house. His feet cracked the leaves an early autumn wind had brought down from the ancient oaks that groved around it. He could smell the broken leaves and the rich exposed soil of the recently harvested fields. He was a quiet man by nature, and thoughtful, and his manner suggested that worry was his habit. Lines were long-drawn between his brows, and sprang from eyes that were deep blue though somewhat dulled by his cares. His dark, waving hair was covered by a two-year-old panama that he had painstakingly cared for so that even now it kept its shape and there was no sweat stain along the black band. He was forty, tall and slender, with long delicate hands that in recent years had developed protective callouses.

He was seen by his neighbors as a rather unhappy man, but while he was serious, and dedicated, he was not without happiness. He had worked long and hard since The Great Depression took the land, not so that he and Annabelle could go on to something better, but simply with the hope that they would be able to resume life at Shadow Oaks as it once was. He had a deep and continuing love for the plantation, and a poignant yearning for life as it was there in his childhood. Even after his parents were gone, in the first years of his marriage, the gentility had prevailed, and it was that softness, that yielding to the wisdom of the past and considered resistance to change, for which he longed.

Maurice was of the firm conviction that he had been able to save Shadow Oaks only by concentrating every minute of every day for the past few years on doing so, and that if anything at any time broke that concentration, the frayed thread by which he held his family home would surely part. He had tended most of the plantation himself, and had managed, through kindness and promises, to hang onto two of his sharecroppers. Their hard work, added to his and that of the able-bodied coloreds that wandered the land searching for day work, had so far been sufficient. Lately Maurice had let himself entertain some small hope that things would soon get better, with Franklin Delano Roosevelt in the first year of his presidency. When the hope entered his mind, he admonished himself to be wary, to maintain his concentration until he was sure.

When he was within the dim morning coolness cast by the trees he raised his eyes to look at his automobile, a Ford sedan, already five years old. He had backed it into the carriage house because it would have to be cranked so the engine would start. He opened the car door, set the choke, got the crank from the floorboards and went to the front. The engine failed to turn over on the first two turns of the crank, but on the third, it chugged loudly twice, coughed with a weary expiration of its breath, and just when Maurice was ready to try again, fired to life. The entire car rocked with the engine's uneven rhythm and Maurice hurried around, jumped inside and adjusted the choke. He let the engine idle to warm up, mindful, all the while, that it was using gasoline. But gasoline was cheap, along with everything else because people of the land had no money with which to buy, and it was important that he make the automobile last as long as possible. It would take time for even Mister Roosevelt to bring the country back to normal.

As he waited, hearing the metallic rattling and gasping of the engine, Maurice rested his gaze on his house, taking into himself its comfort. Even in its current state of disrepair, the West Indies Planter, built by his forefathers over a hundred years earlier, gave him pleasure. It was one of a number of plantation houses raised along the great river about that time, some of them in the grand French Empire and Greek Revival styles, but none of them, Maurice thought, so peculiarly suited to the Mississippi river country as the Planter. The wide veranda that spanned the length of the back was matched by one on the front, and tall shuttered windows opened onto both to let the air soar from front to back through the high-ceilinged rooms. The house sat solidly on an above-the-ground basement as high as a man's head. Four times in his childhood the brown river had crept up to Shadow Oaks to flow through the basement built for just that eventuality.

Perhaps had Maurice Cabot had a close friend, or had he been one to chat idly with Annabelle, he would have put into words his feeling for Shadow Oaks. But it would not have occurred to Maurice Cabot to talk about a second, perhaps even greater source of joy in his otherwise pleasureless life. He would not have, in fact, recognized it as joy, since it was generated by a small boy. A small colored boy. The boy's name was Booker, and he was the five-year-old son of the only servant Maurice had managed to keep for Annabelle. The boy was simply there, underfoot or at his heels as he worked. As a man took pleasure from the tender morning sun and the great blue sky, Maurice took pleasure from Booker, and it was not necessary to recognize the sun, the sky, or the boy as noteworthy gifts from God.

Booker's great worth, though Maurice had never sought to identify it, was a never-failing sweetness and good humor. Every day, in a dozen small ways, Maurice could make Booker happy, as he no longer made anyone else happy, even Annabelle, long-suffering as she might be. Maurice could, without half trying, bring to blossom the beautiful smile on Booker's life-awaiting, joy-expecting face. And Booker's smile was like liquid gold poured over Maurice's worry-sodden day. That the boy was of inestimable value to him was a thought that he had never, and would never, express, for Booker was after all, a boy of color. He was not the son Maurice would have had. He was simply a little nigger boy, the fatherless son of the woman who worked in the kitchen and did the wash.

All this was sensed more than thought while the automobile warmed up, and when it was ready to go, he eased it out of the carriage house onto the shade-dappled drive. He glanced casually toward the cabin that stood a hundred yards away and back from the house, because often when Maurice needed to drive to the store at the junction of two red clay roads several miles distant, Booker would beg to ride along. It was a long drive, and the roads were in bad repair, even at the end of the summer, and having company made it seem shorter. That morning, however, the boy was nowhere to be seen. Maurice neither acknowledged his own small disappointment nor considered calling for Booker.

The car had eased perhaps forty yards along the drive when he saw Booker's head bobbing at the window on the passenger side. He stopped the car and hid his gladness behind a frown. "You could get hurt running long-side a movin' car, boy. That's a foolish thing to do." Maurice spoke slowly, in the manner of the people of Southern Mississippi, drawing out his words as though he loved them too dearly to let go.

"Please, Mist' Mo'rees, lemme ride 'long. Ah wo'n be no bothuh, hones' ah wo'n."

Maurice made the expected objection. "Didn't your mamma give you work to do this mornin', boy?"

"Yessuh."

"And did you finish it?"

"Yessuh."

Booker's eyes were deep caverns that caught the irregular patches of light that fell through the oaks. Tufts of hair velveted his well-shaped skull. His skin, as black as the inside of a closet on a hot day, was sheened with dampness that came from the things that a boy does on a warm southern morning. His smile was meltingly beautiful. In times so stern and hostile as these, such beauty was to be cherished and looking at the boy satisfied some hunger inside of Maurice. He regretted that he no longer felt that gratification when he looked at Annabelle who was a beautiful woman. But, he could not see his wife except through a brown-gray tint of guilt. Annabelle had expected, and rightly so, if not wealth at least a genteel comfort from her marriage, and certainly children, and he had not provided her with either. But, when he looked at Booker, he saw beauty that, in some way, he himself nurtured. For when it came to Booker and his mother, Maurice provided for them as well, and a little better, than law and custom required of him. And so, to Maurice there was, in addition to the boy's beauty, the return of a small self-satisfaction, rare in such difficult times.

"Well, then, Booker, I reckon it wouldn't hurt for you to ride along. Run and tell your mamma so she won't be worryin'."

Booker giggled as he whirled and ran toward the house.

There was a moment, then, when Maurice thought he should have said, 'no.' In an inner part of him was planted, as deep as the seed cane in the field, the knowledge that a man should take care that his Negros kept their place. The thought was so common and familiar that it hardly was expressible and it carried no ill will. It was an inherited part of Maurice, like his mother's hands. It occurred to him, briefly, that in normal times, when there were many colored working around the plantation that he would have been more attentive to such details. But with only Booker and his mother, and with the risk of having his concentration broken for something upon which the survival of Shadow Oaks did not depend, it was of no great concern.

It was only a few moments until the boy burst out of the house and ran toward the automobile, as light as a young rabbit, his bare feet hardly touching the ground, the legs of his bib overalls flapping about his thin brown ankles. Maurice, watching, laughed aloud. Booker smiled, oblivious of the happiness he bestowed, and clambered into the back and perched on the edge of the seat. "Mamma said my overhalls was'n too dirty." Maurice could smell soap. The boy's mother had washed his face and hands. She kept him very clean.

Maurice put the car in gear and drove onto the dusty River Bottom Road. The boy, isolated by his circumstances, was not aware of "his place," and the need to keep to it, and so he kept up a constant stream of questions to his mother's employer. He asked about the countryside, the lovely old homes they passed and the people who lived inside, what Maurice was going to buy at the store, and what every knob and screw he could find in the car was for. Maurice answered him, sometimes, and when he did, then Booker asked more questions based on whatever Maurice said. Maurice couldn't help thinking how quick the child was, and that it was a shame there wasn't much the boy could do with his mental agility. His thoughts were surface ones, skimming along the stream of his mind, evaporating quickly, and Booker's eager, husky voice wisped through them like mist raised by sunrise. When he wanted to know what it was that grew in a field they were passing, Maurice was reminded to worry about whether he would have to sell off a piece of ground for enough cash to make it through the winter. If he was going to have to, anyhow, he ought to do it now, before the market was glutted in the spring. Thinking about selling even a handful of the black soil of Shadow Oaks caused a wrenching in his stomach.

His worry was interrupted by Booker. "Mist' Mo'rees?...kin ah set up in the front seat?"

"What would you want to do that for, Booker?"

"Ah don' know. Ah jus' want to."

"'Just want to' is no good reason, boy." Maurice, still fretful about the selling of the land, was putting little thought into what he was saying.

There was a pause. "Well, then, Mist' Mo'rees, ah guess ah want to set up on the front seat so's ah can see how you drive this automobile. You jus' about the bes' driver in the county, Mist' Mo'rees."

Maurice laughed. He'd been bested, and being bested by Booker brought a small, unexpected flush of pride. "All right, Booker. You remember now, you'll have to get in the back before we get to the store." The remark came from the same taken-for-granted place inside Maurice where the need for colored to know their place was stored, and it was not even noted by Booker. He scrambled over the back of the front seat and sat beside Maurice.

As the road climbed out of the black bottom land to the red clay of the low hills the smells that reached Maurice's nostrils changed from the dark fecundity of the fall-plowed farmland to the dusty, piney odor of the woods. They rounded a curve and Maurice saw the store ahead in the middle of a clearing that had been carved out beside the road. The old store itself was barely surviving the hard times, and that its doors were still open was to the credit of the store-keeper, Willard Henry, whose father had passed it down to him.

The building was an unpainted frame structure that had taken on the brick red color of the earth around it. The front was nearly covered with rusty tin signs: *Coca-Cola, the Pause that Refreshes; Prince Albert; Calumet Baking Powder*. The store stood on a foundation of tall six-by-six posts so that the porch that ran the full width, maybe forty feet, could serve as a loading dock for flour and chicken mash. At the far end of it Maurice could see the top half of a Phillips gasoline pump, the amber colored liquid barely visible through the dirty glass. Along that edge of the porch lay a few tools that Willard or his customers used to fix flat tires and make other minor mechanical repairs. A crude set of steps, red with dirt, rose from the trampled ground up to the center of the porch, and directly across were the double screen doors that led into the dim interior of the store. A heavy homemade wooden bench sat against the wall to the left of the doors.

On the bench sat four men, and another stood at one end with his foot resting on it, one fist curled on his raised knee.

All of them wore overalls, some blue faded almost white, some striped. They had on wide-brimmed straw hats, gone shapeless and ragged-edged, except for one who wore a rail-road cap, striped like his overalls. Those who didn't have a plug of tobacco in their cheeks at that moment carried the stains that proved the habit on the stubble of their chins and the fronts of their overalls. On their feet were heavy, mud-and-manure-chunked high-top work shoes, the laces whipped through bright brass hooks at the top. All of them stared coldly at the car as Maurice pulled up in front, slowly, so as not to raise a dust.

The men on the porch were the poor whites who dirt farmed wherever they could, living in shacks with their sickly, worn-out wives and dirty children. Two of them, Maurice knew, were bootleggers, and he had no idea how the others managed to feed themselves and their families. While he'd seen all of them before, he knew the names of only one or two. Maurice used the worries and concerns of his own life to avoid thinking about such people for it pained him to know that women and children lived in squalor, and it made him angry that there were men like these who appeared not to care enough to do anything about it.

He turned off the engine and leaned forward to peer up through the windshield and nod grudgingly at the silent little group on the bench. It was at that moment that he remembered, too late, that Booker still sat on the front seat beside him. He might not have remembered it at all except for the eyes of the men. When he realized why they were looking at him in that way his heart unexpectedly jumped. He was somewhat embarrassed that he had been caught with a nigger boy in the front seat of his car, and the embarrassment was deepened because the lapse had been noticed by such sorry men. He didn't know whether he ought to scold Booker and make him climb over into the back seat or just ignore the situation. It didn't amount to anything, anyway, so he decided to ignore it as if it wasn't worth his attention.

He said to Booker, "Stay in the car, now, I just have to get some picklin' spices for Miz Cabot, and I'll be back in just a minute."

As he spoke to Booker he reached with his left hand to open his door. He jumped as it slammed back against the latch. A shadow had fallen over the window. Maurice turned his head to see two fleshy, freckled hands on the window frame. His anger flared like a struck match, but he didn't particularly want to have words with anybody, so he held himself in check. He let his gaze climb slowly over the filthy bib of Hube Coler's overalls, past the open collar of his dirty shirt that revealed scanty, sandy-colored chest hair and on up to Hube's face. He was a big man, and fleshy, and his broad face, not recently shaved, was dominated by small, almost colorless eyes. He wasn't smiling, and there was a glint behind his eyes, that in spite of Maurice's determination not to get into anything with anybody, bothered him. A small knot of dis-ease formed in his belly. "Mornin', Hube," Maurice said.

Coler kept his position and for a few seconds didn't say anything at all. When he did speak, his voice, even though it was coarse with back-county accent, was soft. "Who's that fine-lookin' boy riding in the front seat o' yo' Ford, Mister Cabot? My, my, don' he look fancy, ridin' rat up there in the front seat lak white folks?"

Maurice couldn't think of what to say, and so he was silent too long before he looked up at Coler. "I'm ready to get out of the car now, Hube," he said. The man's breath smelled of bad teeth. Maurice waited for him to move back and when he didn't, feigned a heartiness he didn't feel and said, "Got to pick up some picklin' spices for Miz Cabot, Hube. They're picklin' peaches this mornin'." He glanced at the other men, sitting up there on the bench, watching, grinning.

After what seemed to Maurice a long time, Coler stepped back, but not very far, and very slowly. The grin clung to the broad face and his eyes didn't leave Maurice's. Maurice glanced at Booker. The boy's eyes were enormous and, before Maurice could grab him, he flipped around and almost clambered over the back of the seat before Maurice grabbed at his overalls and pulled him back. Maurice surprised himself by what he did and said next. Clamping his hand over the boy's wrist, he said, "You stay where you are, Booker." Booker looked up at him, confused, and Maurice, moved by his own quick anger, leaned toward the boy and said firmly, "I'll be in the store for just a minute, Booker. I'll be right back. Now you just sit here and don't pay a bit of attention to anybody. Don't you even look at anybody. Hear me?" Booker's eyes darted back and forth between Maurice's. "You understand that now, Booker?" Booker nodded. "All right, now you do what I said, and I'll bring you something." Not even that brought a smile to Booker's face, and Maurice, his breath leaving him, could see that the boy, too, had sensed the oily weight of threat in the humid air.

Coler still stood so close to the car that when Maurice got out, he had to push awkwardly past him, feeling the soft bulge of the big belly. He was determined not to look at Coler, but, still feeling obliged, as the better of the two, to take responsibility for preventing unpleasantness, he said, as he started up the steps, "How's the family, Hube?"

"W'y they fine, Mister Cabot. My two big strappin' boys, they 'specially fine." There was a pause and then the coarse voice went on, slow and insinuating, "Maybe this 'year nigger boy gonna grow into a fine big strappin' boy, too, so's y'all have something' to be proud of."

There was a burst of laughter from the bench and one of the men slapped his knee. Maurice hesitated with one foot on the top step to the porch. All at one he was weary. He didn't have the desire or the energy to expend on an argument. If he was a better man than Hube Coler, then he had to act like it. He stepped onto the porch and drew himself tall. Smiling the best casual, friendly smile he knew how, he said to the others, "Mornin', boys. I hope things are going well with youall."

One or two of them muttered something, and one leaned forward and spat tobacco juice through his teeth...*ssst!*...on the floor between his feet. Two of the others continued to stare at Maurice, big wide mocking smiles on their faces.

Maurice touched the brim of his hat with his hand and said, "Well, mornin' boys," and was reaching for the handle on the screen door when he was stopped by Coler's voice from below.

"Y'all ought to git yourself a new car, Mister Cabot. How about one of them new V-8s? Ah'm s'prised, a man owns a big fancy place like Shada' Oaks drivin' around in a beat-up ol' car like this'n. W'y, folks'd think you cain't afford nothin' better."

With effort, Maurice maintained his silence. Of all of the people of the South, he thought, as he'd never stopped to think before, these were the lowest kind, and he could see now, clearly, why everybody, including the Negroes, looked down on them. None of the men even knew how to talk with decent people, and trying to disabuse Hube Coler of his bad manners was a waste of good time. Such men, ill-born and ignorant, would seize on any little opportunity, when they had the advantage of numbers, to insult decent folks. That he had to swallow a stupid and silly insult from one of them made him sick, and when the thought that it was embarrassment he was feeling, not righteousness, came into his mind, he was impatient and shook it off. He sighed, getting ahold of himself, and said, "Times are hard, Hube." His own voice seemed to loosen his intelligence, and he added, deftly, "But things are going to get better for all of us now, with Mister Roosevelt in the White House." He heard murmurs of agreement from the row of men on the bench and thought that he had put an end to the contentiousness.

A glance at Coler showed him he'd failed. The man's face was no longer taunting, but angry and bitter. His massive jaw clenched and he said, "Ain't nobody ever goin' to hep the likes of us, and y'all and y'all's kind goin' to see they don't."

Maurice hadn't expected such venom from the man. Smallness, yes, and the surly peevishness, but not the unclothed hate that stung him from the little watery eyes. He frowned and shook his head slightly. Something deeper, something Maurice couldn't quite grasp was eating Hube

Coler. Then, as a jolt of fine bourbon on a cold day permeates the very marrow of a man's bones, the knowledge came home to him: to the sorry man before him, Maurice Cabot was one of the privileged; one of those fate had dealt the upper hand. Maurice Cabot was a "have," and Hube Coler and the others were the "have nots." The hate he saw in Coler's face and the hopeless, given-up eyes of the others on the bench was the hate of the classless for those of class, and it was almost incomprehensible to Maurice, entrapped for so long and so entirely in his own life and death struggle to save the plantation and its way of life. And even as he tried to comprehend and accept, the further truth came to him...compared with their own poverty-damaged children, the little Negro child, too, was privileged, and, in the end, it was that they could not bear.

The strange new knowledge filled Maurice so that he felt swollen under his skin. For part of an instant, there was pity, but the emotion was stillborn, killed by an older, dominating cautiousness that dwelt inside him. He felt the hairs on his forearms raise as he realized this wasn't the game of a schoolyard bully. He quieted a quick spurt of panic and, in a fit of desperation, turned back to Coler. "Well, Hube, all of us want the best for everybody. And I do think that the president cares for all Americans. Things are going to get better, Hube. I can almost guarantee you that."

One of the men on the bench said, "Yeah, things got to git better. They sure as hell cain't get no worse." The others nodded their heads, but none of them looked up.

Maurice began to draw in a breath of relief, but it caught in his throat when Coler's face changed again, and he could see that Coler hadn't wanted the others to agree with him. He narrowed his eyes, stared hard at Maurice for a moment, then his face relaxed as he moved the subject back to more comfortable territory. "Well, now, Mo'rees,"...Maurice noted that Coler had dropped the "mister" and was using his first name..."ah don' know about all that. But what ah *do* know is that y'all got yoursef a mighty fancy little nigger boy here in the front seat of yo' car."

Maurice's voice was indecisive. He said, weakly, "Yes, Booker's a nice boy." The only thing that made sense was for him to just go in to the store and get Annabelle's spices and get in the car and go on home without saying another word. He moved quickly, leaning down so he could see Booker's face inside the car and said, "I'll be back in just a jiffy, Booker. You wait, now, you hear?" Without waiting for the boy to answer, or looking at anybody, he hurried into the store. Willard Henry was just walking behind the big counter and Maurice knew from the look on his face that he had been watching and listening.

"Annabelle needs some picklin' spices, Willard. She's waitin', so I'd better get on back as quick as I can. Oh, and I'd better have a licorice whip, too, I guess."

Willard, usually a talker, was silent. He went around the counter to a shelf and came back with the can of spices. "That'll be nineteen cents, Maurice, and a penny for the licorice. You want it on your bill?" He put the spices and the candy in a small paper sack.

"I don't guess so, Willard. Not this time." He gave the storekeeper a little smile, but Willard didn't smile back. Maurice laid down a quarter and when the storekeeper put his change on the old counter, blackened by oil and the stroking of generations of hands, he said, "Well, thanks, Willard. Say 'hello' to Miz Henry for us."

The screen door squawked when he opened it. Keeping his eyes on his feet, he went down the steps. Coler had moved to the near side of the car and stood close to the passenger door. Maurice slipped between the front of the car and the porch, and went around to the driver's window. He took the licorice out of the paper sack, leaned in through the window and gave it to Booker then tossed the sack into the back seat. He set the magneto and choke, got the crank, and went to the front of the car. He was relieved when it started on the first turn. Quickly he got inside and was just forcing the shift lever into place when Hube Coler opened the door next to Booker.

He said, "Git out h'year boy. Let's git a good look at y'all."

Booker looked to Maurice for guidance but before Maurice could tell him to stay where he was so he could get the car moving, Hube had yanked the door all the way open and pulled the boy out. Booker was trembling, and Maurice saw he was about to cry.

Maurice said, "Now, you let go of him, Hube. He's got things to do this mornin', and I have, too." Coler continued to hold Booker by the arm and grin down at him. Maurice checked the choke, and, leaving the car running, got out and went around to them. A low, skulking dread worked in his bowels. He reached for Booker's arm, but Coler brushed his hand away like he was shooing gnats.

Coler bent down, resting his hands, big and round as cantaloupes, on his bent knees, and put his face close to Booker's. Then he laughed. Maurice saw Booker flinch, and he put his hand out again, but Coler swung his arm, forcing Maurice back.

Coler laughed again loudly, plainly for the benefit of the men on the bench, and said, "Boys, ah jis' don't think that this h'year's even Mo'rice's nigger. W'y this boy's too black for you to be his daddy, Mo'rice." Suddenly he was half-dragging Booker up the steps. He stood him before the row of men. Booker was crying but he didn't try to run. Coler said, "Whadya' think, boys? This look like Mo'rice Cabot's boy to y'all?" He turned and grinned down at Maurice still standing beside the car. "W'y, Mo'rice, it looks like you ain't never fathered even a nigger boy. This one's pure. Pure, un-die-luted nigger." His eyes were cold all at once, and he spoke through the rotten teeth. "So how come the little black bastard was ridin' in the front seat of yo' goddamned car?"

Somehow the insult to his manhood, because it was as stupid and crude as the man who hurled it, calmed Maurice. More than anything else, he was disgusted. Poor little Booker was crying in earnest. All Maurice wanted to do was get Booker and go home. He moved along the ground at the edge of the high porch and thought that if he reached up and grabbed at Booker quickly enough, he could get them both into the car that was still running, and go on home. He timed his move carefully, but Coler was too fast. He jerked the boy away, picked him up like a sack of flour and ran, his huge body bouncing with every step, to the far end of the long porch. "Y'all want 'im, y'all come and git 'em."

Fear, shaming fear, swallowed up Maurice's disgust. He tried to keep his knees steady as he climbed the steps and walked over to Coler. He put out his arms for Booker and Booker reached for him and whimpered, but Coler's hamlike hands were clasped around Booker's slender belly. Maurice tried to put some force in his voice when he said, "All right, Coler, you've had your fun now. You're right, I ought not to have put the boy in the front seat. It was just a mistake. Now, give him to me."

Coler's grin turned into a low, satisfied chuckle. Then, quickly, he stepped to one side and hollered, "Ketch, boys!" and as he did, threw Booker across the porch. One of the men at the other end leapt up from the bench and caught the boy and bound him tight with his arms.

Shock bolted through Maurice. He ran for Booker, but in the instant before he reached him, Coler shouted, "Here...th'ow 'im back to me!" and the man lifted the little boy high over his head and threw him over Maurice. Maurice's watched and felt sick at his stomach. He could hear the mens' loud, ugly laughter over Booker's screams. He was scared for the boy. If they missed and threw him off of the high porch, he could be badly hurt, or even killed. And he was afraid for himself.

The men laughed and stamped their feet and Maurice ran toward Booker again, and again the child was thrown high in the air. Looking up Maurice saw the length of Booker's torso writhing and his little arms and legs flying about helplessly. He still gripped his licorice and it twirled like a dead garter snake.

The men had taken up positions around the porch and Maurice ran from one end to the other like a ballplayer caught between bases. His breathing had become hard and coarse and each intake made a rough, raspy sound. Booker's body went higher and higher, and Maurice saw it against the brilliant, innocent blue sky. He darted and turned, trying desperately to intercept the child. Over the noise of his own breathing, Booker's wails and the laughter of the men, Maurice heard the engine of his car chug and die, and with it went the last of his pathetic hope that he could catch the boy and escape.

He caught a glance of Booker's face. It was wet with tears and smeared with snot, and his screams were broken up by great, tearing sobs that shuddered through the little body. The sounds cut Maurice like a serrated knife dragging over his bones. He jumped as high as he could, trying to reach the flying body, and when he missed, he fell on the rough wood planking, tearing his pants and soiling his white shirt with red dirt. He had lost his hat, and his knee was bleeding. He was close to crying, himself, with frustration and fright and humiliation.

Maurice Cabot was helpless. Powerless. He had lost control of the events around him. His heart pounded violently as his eyes shot from face to grinning face, and as he looked at the men, a deep, hot hate boiled up in him. The force of it amazed him. Suddenly his eye caught the tools that lay against the front of the store and he darted to them and picked up the tire iron. He started for Hube Coler, the heavy weapon raised. In the eye of his mind, he saw the tire iron coming down directly in the center of Hube Coler's head and crushing his great stupid skull. The image was deeply satisfying, and he almost smiled. He was so focused on his intent that, when, in the split-second before the weapon crashed down on Coler's head, his hand was caught from behind, he wasn't sure what had happened. He shook his head to clear it. He had been in the act of killing Hube Coler, and suddenly it was ended and Coler, inexplicably, stood before him, alive.

The man who had grabbed Maurice's hand wrested the tire iron away and threw it off the porch, and a second man kicked the other tools to the ground and the game resumed. Booker's body sailed through the air, again and again. But the game had taken on a different tone. Quieter. The laughter had stopped. The men were concentrating on their techniques. Higher they threw the child. Faster.

Maurice forced himself to stop running and stood, exhausted, his knees trembling, in the center of the porch. He drew in deep breaths, sought for and located his reason. He set his jaw, clenched his hands at his sides and faced Coler. And Coler, seeing the change in him, caught the boy and held him. Maurice said, his voice low and strong, "You give me that boy or I'll call the sheriff on you, you bootlegging bastard!"

The coarse call of a crow cut the silence. Maurice's fear was gone. Slowly, very slowly, he walked toward Coler. He was close, only three or four feet away, when Coler reached down and pulled out a pocket knife. He put it to his mouth, and with his teeth, opened it. "This h'year is my whittlin' knife. It's sharp enough to gut this boy with one stroke."

Maurice stopped. His heart hit his throat so hard he almost coughed. Coler, in control again, sucked in his breath and grinned. "Y'all such a fine nigger-lovin' landowner, Mo'rice, y'all think y'own ever'thang. Well, y'don't own me, Mo'rice, and y'don' own the rest o' the boys, do he, boys?"

Maurice heard a murmur, but then a single voice drawled, "Aw, hell, Hube, let it go." By drawing the knife on a child, Coler had gone too far even for his own kind. Behind Maurice there was a shuffling, and two of the men went down the steps and walked away without looking back.

Coler watched them, and Maurice saw rage rise to his face. He turned to Maurice and his jowls quivered when he said, "Y'all come one step closer and ah'll cut this boy's ear off sure as hell. Y'hear me, Cabot?" The wide doughy face had purpled and the small eyes narrowed. Booker, imprisoned, sobbed.

Maurice's chest ached with love for the little boy. Surely somewhere inside Hube Coler there was shred of human decency to which he could appeal. He said, "Please Coler, give me the boy. You all have come out ahead. You had your fun and made a fool out of me. That's what you wanted. Now, I'd be obliged if you would give me the boy."

Suddenly Booker reached both arms out to Maurice and wailed, "Help me, Mist' Mo'rees. *Help me!*" and involuntarily Maurice stepped forward and reached for him. Astonishingly fast for a man of his size, Coler set the boy on his feet, pulled one of Booker's ears taut and placed the edge of the knife against it. The sun flashed off the blade. Maurice retreated.

Coler grinned. "How j'all like to have a fancy little nigger boy that's got only one ear, Mistah High 'n Mighty?"

Maurice swallowed. When he spoke, his voice was husky and to his shame, it shook. "Look, Coler, you're going too far. I could get the law onto you for this. Now give me the boy and we'll just forget all of this ever happened."

Coler laughed. "Well, now, it don't matter none what happens now, 'cause ah ain't never goin' to let nobody fergit. Ever'body's goin' to know how Mo'rice Cabot, the fine owner of Shada' Oaks Plantation, crawled at the feet of Hube Coler. Now, maybe I'll give you the boy if you crawl over here to me, Mister Mo'rice Cabot. But if y'all think you too good for crawlin', w'y then we'll jis have to rid this boy o' one o' his black ears."

Suddenly the doors of the store burst open. Willard Henry stood in the doorway with a shotgun aimed at Coler's face. The other two men remaining on the porch scurried down the steps and hurried away.

"Let loose o' the boy, Hube," Henry said.

Coler whirled to face him, and as he did, the blade of the knife slipped through the stretched tissue of Booker's ear lobe. The little boy screamed and blood spurted over Coler's hand, but he hung on. He stared into the barrel of the gun and his face twitched. "This ain't none of y'all's goddamned bid'ness, Henry."

"You're on my property, Coler. Let loose o' the boy."

The air cracked and popped with the energy of the conflict.

Coler's gaze snapped from Willard and the shotgun to Maurice and back. He gritted his teeth and gave a final tug on the wounded ear that sent Booker's blood spattering, and pushed him toward Maurice. Maurice wrapped his arms around the child and stroked the bloodied head. Much later it seemed to him, Coler lowered his hand, wiped the blood from the knife on his pantsleg and, his bull-like head lowered, walked past Maurice and Booker and went down the steps.

Booker's crying went on but Maurice couldn't see to him yet. Not yet because he could not take his eyes off the retreating figure. Twice Coler turned back as if he would return and finish whatever awful job he had planned in his small mind, but Willard Henry stood, the gun cradled in his arms, returning Coler's looks. Coler walked down the road, turned to look back once more, his hands fisted at his sides, then went out of sight around a curve.

Maurice knelt before Booker. "Let me see, Booker. Let me see." He inspected the cut as well as he could through the blood. The lobe of Booker's ear had been cleanly slit where it joined his head, and blood still poured from it, but Maurice could see it would heal all right. He took his handkerchief to it, but it was quickly soaked.

Still trying to wipe the wound dry, he said, "Willard, get me something to clean him up with, will you, please?" To Booker he said, "You're going to be all right, Booker. He didn't cut off your ear. It's all there." He looked around for the cloth that he expected Willard to bring him to clean the boy with, but the storekeeper hadn't moved. Maurice stood up. "I ought to clean the blood off of the boy, Willard. Could you find me a clean rag or something?"

Willard Henry's eyes were as cold as Coler's had been. "Y'all git the hell out of here, Cabot. You're goddamned lucky you didn't get somebody killed. You and your sonofabitchin' little nigger boy. Now, I said go on home." He turned to go inside, then hesitated and looked back at Maurice. More quietly he said, "Dammit, Maurice, it's people like you keep opening the doors just a little tiny bit that's going to bring trouble down on all of us. Cain't you see that when you crack that door, one of these days they going to stick their foot in it, and all of 'em...*all* of 'em at once goin' to come in on us? That's jis' what they're waitin' for. Just a crack in the door.

Now go on home. Take Annabelle her picklin' spices. Go on now." He went inside and the door swung shut behind him.

Maurice stared after him, startled and confused. What in the world was Willard talking about? Booker was just a little boy. And having him in the front seat was such a little, unimportant thing. And Booker the same as *belonged* to Maurice. He *had* to take care of him. He didn't have any choice. Couldn't Willard see that?

He felt Booker tugging at his pants and, still bewildered by the storekeeper's words, he bent and picked up the boy and carried him down the steps to the car. He gave him the bloody handkerchief and told him to hold it against his ear, then he cranked the car, got inside, and drove away.

A mile down the road, he pulled to the side and stopped. In the back seat he had some rags he kept in case he had to wipe the windshield, and he got them and then went around and got Booker out of the car.

Maurice sat down on the running board and stood Booker in front of him and began to tend to the ear. The blood was beginning to clot, and he touched the black skin tenderly. The boy had stopped crying but still sucked in deep convulsive sobs. Maurice said, "It'll stop hurting pretty soon now, Booker."

"Yessuh, Mist' Mo'rees."

*"Yessuh, Mist' Mo'rees."* The words stung. Booker called him 'sir.' Even after Maurice had failed him. Even after men whose skins were the same as Maurice's had commited acts of physical and emotional brutality on his innocent child's mind and body. Feeling the hot flush of shame, he saw himself as Booker, and Coler and the others, had seen him, running crazily back and forth across the porch, falling, tearing his pants, losing his hat, scraping his knee, laughed at and held, weak and helpless. Maurice could hardly bear the images and he swallowed sick saliva that flowed into his mouth. But even if Maurice had lost respect for himself, the child still said, "yes, sir." That the little Negro child knew no other way brought a gray sadness down on Maurice, and in it was the first tiny seed of doubt that his way, and the way of his

forefathers, was the right way. Maurice searched the little face before him, and almost said the words, *"Don't call me 'sir'"* before he saw the danger. He sagged against the car door, his heart swollen with sadness for himself and tenderness for the child. He had almost told a little colored boy not to call a white man 'sir.' Would some day some other white man spill Booker's blood again because he didn't say 'Yessuh'?

He rested his head against the car and closed his eyes. He released a long, weary breath, and with it, his strength drained out of him. He was exhausted from the terrible day. He had failed to hold himself above worthless men, and he knew the story would soon spread over the countryside. He had broken faith with Willard Henry, and, he could see now, with all his friends and neighbors. Annabelle would be shamed, and he was deeply sorry for that. Even Booker's mother would hate him now, for letting her boy ride in the front seat of a white man's car so that some other white man would use that for a reason to cut him with a knife.

And there was the final thing, the greater thing, that Maurice Cabot had learned about himself that day. It sapped his strength. The remembrance of a violent Maurice Cabot. Pressed beyond enduring by helplessness and humiliation, Maurice Cabot would have killed. He, who had never before raised his hand with violent intent, would have killed a man. He recognized, not fleetingly, but fully and so that it would always remain with him, what it meant to be powerless. In that moment he saw, clearly and terribly, how powerlessness stretched beyond the point of human tolerance, eventually and inevitably, takes on a power of its own that is violence.

In a few seconds all his sensibilities, the half-formed balances of right and wrong, and the never-finalized image of himself as a man, whipped about and through his mind like a hurricane. He turned to the child as if there he could find the explanation that would calm the winds of his torment and pulled the little boy to him. It felt so good to hold the child. He was comforted but then the boy stiffened against the unusual show of emotion. The child was made uneasy by the Maurice who held him, a strange man he didn't know. To comfort him, Maurice pushed him away and smiled. But he couldn't hold the smile and he began to cry, pressing his face against the small, bony shoulder of the boy. He cried for himself and for Booker, and for a way of life that now seemed dirtied. His tears wet the boy's bloody shirt and the child became frightened. He said, "Don' cry, Mist' Mo'rees. How come y'all cryin'?"

"It's nothing, Booker. Nothing," he said and raised his head and turned away to wipe his eyes with his hand.

But the boy, warned by something born in him, didn't believe the man. He began to look up and down the road and Maurice, watching him, realized that he searched for every child's great fear. The unknown. The unseen. "Is sumthin' out there, Mist' Mo'rees? Is sumthin' goin' to git us?"

An intake of breath shook Maurice as if he, too, had been sobbing for hours. And because neither the man he had been, nor the man he had become that day could leave a child's fear unassuaged, he arranged a calmness on his own face and said, "No, Booker." He smiled at the little boy. "Of course not. Nothin's going to get us now. We're safe. We're going to be just fine now."

But Maurice Cabot's heart said, "Yes, Booker." He put his face aginst the little shoulder again and his heart whispered, "Yes, Booker. There's something out there. And, yes, child, some day it's going to get us. I don't know how much it's going to hurt, or even if, in the end, it will be bad or good. But, yes, Booker, one day...one day...somethin's goin' to git us."

# A Family In Winter

Mildred pushed the car door open with her elbow, and holding the baby tightly against her, pulled a corner of the well-washed blanket over his head against the cold Oklahoma wind. With her foot she felt for the running board and carefully stepped to the frozen ground.

Motioning with her head toward the back seat of the car, she said, "You get her, Samuel. And bring the paper sack." Without looking back she hurried over patches of yellow frost-bitten grass to the weather-worn house on a narrow lot next to a metal shop. Still protecting the baby from the wind, she struggled through the door. It seemed colder inside than out.

In the bedroom she put the baby down, folded the blanket back and looked at the tiny pale face. The child stared back at his mother with great dark somber eyes.

After a moment, Mildred straightened her shoulders and pulled herself erect. There was no need to feel guilty about what the doctor said. If her milk had failed to fill the baby's stomach, if he was suffering from malnutrition, it was not her fault. Things had been too hard for her. In the comfort of her thoughts, Mildred became calm and her face took on a peaceful and pious expression. If it be the will of God, and with the strength of Jesus Christ in her, she would nurse her baby back to health. First, as the old doctor had suggested, the baby would have ice cream every day. She would hold back enough from Samuel's pay envelope to buy a nickel's worth each day, and the baby would have his nourishment.

Her thoughts were interrupted by voices from the front room. Samuel was talking and the child was laughing. As Mildred took off her heavy black woolen coat and hung it in the closet she felt a rush of anger. Even at a time like this, when they had just learned that their son was starving, Samuel could find time to play with the girl. Make her squeal with delight. Mildred listened, her mouth tight. She heard her husband say, "There! Are you Daddy's little princess?"

"Me Daddy's princess. Daddy's princess!" The child's high voice sliced through Mildred and she winced.

"Samuel," she called, pulling her good dark blue rayon dress over her head, "light the stove. It's too cold in here for the baby." She slipped the dress on a hanger and took her cotton housedress off a hook. "And make her put her coat away."

Mildred sourly avoided calling her daughter by her name. Such a silly, frivolous name for a child. Many times she had regretted telling Samuel he could choose the name when the girl was born three years ago. He had seemed so delighted, and immediately said they would call her "Bobbie."

"Roberta. That's nice," she had said.

"No! Not Roberta. Just Bobbie," he had insisted. Weak from a long and difficult labor, and dazed with exhaustion, Mildred had simply turned her head away.

Sometimes it seemed to her that it was the name that kept her from feeling the way she thought she would about her first child. In the weeks that followed her birth, the little girl grew fat and bright, her eyes changed from the smoky indigo of the infant to their clear, twinkling blue, and her hair lightened and curled. And she laughed. She laughed when her daddy talked baby-talk to her. She laughed at the brilliant white cotton boles blowing in the wind. When Samuel sang to her, she laughed. And before she was able to sit up alone, she laughed aloud at the dancing reflection of her bath water that the bright prairie sun cast on the ceiling above her.

In her daydreams before the birth of the child, Mildred had imagined sweet smiles and the beautiful cooing sounds babies make. But she had not imagined her baby laughing aloud, and the first time she had drawn back swiftly from the child with an unpleasant feeling of surprise. Laughing was for coarse girls. Her child could never be coarse and vulgar.

What Mildred heard in the baby's laughter opened a dark place deep within her and the memories poured in. *She* had laughed. *Lucille* had laughed and laughed. Loudly and raucously. Even when she had done that terrible thing to the rest of them, even in those awful, shameful weeks, Lucille had still found things to laugh about. And now, Mildred's baby—her hair golden and curling, like Lucille's—her eyes blue and sparkling, like Lucille's—laughed. Unexpectedly. Inappropriately. Remembering that she had laughed aloud during the minister's closing prayer on Sunday, Mildred's cheeks burned and she closed her teeth hard together. With disgust she recalled the stupid doting smile on Samuel's face as he looked around proudly to see if people were watching.

Mildred's thin hands worked at the buttons down the front of her dress. Then, before she was finished, the child rushed through the bedroom door, gasping and screaming. "No, no, Daddy! No...don't let the ol' bear get me!"

Samuel was on his knees, after her, his face screwed into an absurd snarl, making a growling noise in his throat.

Mildred whirled away from them, closing the gaping front of the dress over her cotton brassiere. "For goodness sake, Samuel! Don't be so silly. Don't you know you will scare the baby?"

Bobbie's squeals stopped abruptly and her eyes widened. She looked from mother to father. Sheepishly, Samuel got to his feet. Without speaking, he picked up Bobbie and went back to the front room.

Her dress fastened properly, Mildred smoothed her straight black hair toward the bun on her neck. "Is it warm enough in there now for me to feed the baby, Samuel?" she called.

"I guess so," his voice came back to her, expressionless.

Mildred bent over the baby on the bed and the hardness left her face. Here was her son. In his large solemn eyes she saw her own long chin reflected. His soft dark hair the color of her own grew back from his high forehead, just as hers did. He was *her* child. A child who almost never cried, who slept through the night from the very first, and who had not yet laughed aloud, though he was months older than the girl was when she first laughed. Sometimes in the evenings when Samuel was listening to Lum and Abner on his radio, Mildred held her son in her arms while she read her Bible. Often on those evenings, she remembered the picture of the Virgin Mary and the Baby Jesus that hung in her father's house. It was in those moments that she felt herself complete.

She gathered up the baby in his blanket and went into the front room where the little open-front gas heater blazed. Propping the bundle carefully into the corner of the overstuffed chair, she looked sternly at Bobbie who was sitting on the floor playing with a Teddy Bear with no eyes.

"Now don't you touch him, do you hear me?"

The little girl looked at her mother but did not answer.

Samuel said, "Yes, Mildred. I'll see that she doesn't touch him." He didn't look up from his newspaper.

"Where did you put it?" she asked.

"The sack? It's on the cabinet." He followed her into the kitchen.

Mildred opened a cabinet door thick with many coats of white paint and found a small bowl. Samuel was taking the carton out of the rattling paper when Bobbie ran into the room, her shoes clattering on the linoleum floor. When she saw the carton she began to squeal. "Ice c'eam...I want ice c'eam!"

Mildred whirled about, her face distorted. "Be quiet! Stop screaming!"

Samuel looked at the little girl and went to his wife's side and reached past her for another bowl, saying, "I'll fix a little dish for her."

"No! Samuel, you won't! We would never have ice cream in this house at all if the doctor hadn't said the baby needs it. *She* doesn't *need* ice cream. And I won't have you spoiling her any more than you already have."

"But Mildred, she's just a baby herself. She won't understand."

Mildred faced him, her eyes flashing. "Samuel, it's you who doesn't understand! The Lord never meant for our lives to be easy. It's time she learned that she can't have everything just because she's"...Mildred's lip curled and she tipped her head to the side sarcastically..."Daddy's little princess." She turned back to the cabinet and opened the carton. "The trouble is, you think if she's not chattering and babbling and squealing and"...again she twisted her head and simpered the word... *"laughing*...then something's wrong."

"Look Mildred, she's just being a normal, happy little girl."

Mildred's voice rose. "She doesn't *need* to be happy!" She stopped and her eyes widened. Her hand started toward her mouth but then she clinched her fist and put it at her side. After a pause she raised her long chin defiantly and said, "I mean...."

"I guess I know what you mean, Mildred." Samuel's eyes narrowed with anger, then slowly the expression changed to one of sadness. Still looking at his wife, he said quietly, "Bobbie, you run and get your coat, honey. We'll walk down to the store."

Bobbie's face brightened and she began to jump up and down, clapping her hands and yelling, "Daddy, Daddy, can I have candy?"

Mildred spun around. "I said quit screaming!" she shrieked. "Stop it! That's just what the doctor meant. He said I was too nervous to have enough milk for my baby, and it's because of her!" She raised her arm stiffly in front of her and pointed her finger directly at the little girl. Her own voice had become a scream. "She makes me so nervous I could die!"

Quietly Samuel said, "Go on, Bobbie, get your coat and cap on." The child had backed against the kitchen wall and stood there with her finger in her mouth, her eyes big with confusion and fear. At her father's words, she edged toward the door then turned and ran.

Samuel stared at his wife. A muscle under his eye twitched but when he spoke, it was with deadly calm.

"That's it, isn't it? The fact is, you don't like Bobbie." He was silent while the enormity of what he knew filled the room. Then, his voice barely audible, he said, "For Christ' sake, Mildred. She's your own child!"

"She is *not,*" Mildred cried. "I mean she's not *like* me. She's like...*her.* She's like Lucille."

Then, as Samuel stared, trying to comprehend, Mildred turned her back on her husband and let the suppressed anger and hatred surge through her. Bracing her hands hard against the cabinet top, she closed her eyes and savored the luxury of it. She lowered her head and let the scenes tumble before her, one after the other. Like Lucille. Like the sister who with her laughter and pretty face had taken so much of their father's love that there was none left. None left for Mildred. Even when Mildred was the one who cared for him—baked the biscuits he loved—washed and starched and ironed his clothes—scrubbed his house. And then, when Lucille had committed the worst sin of all, and Mildred knew, at last, that her adored father would turn his back on the golden-haired Jezebel and see, for the first time, Mildred's true worth—even then, when they had to tell people that Aunt Hester in Kansas City was sick and needed help and Lucille would have to go to her for a few months—even then, when everybody *knew* and the humiliation was almost unbearable, he had said only that Lucille had made a mistake and needed their love. The final embittering acceptance came to Mildred only after Lucille was gone and she had her father all to herself. Then she waited for him to notice how she, Mildred, cared for him. But his grief for her sister was too great. He never even knew that Mildred loved him best.

The tips of her fingers were white where they pressed against the painted wood of the cabinet top. Her body was rigid. Samuel was beside her, close, trying to see into her face. Even so, she heard his voice from a great distance. "My God, Mildred, you don't even *want* her!"

Mildred struggled to come back. She drew in long, deep breaths. Very slowly she raised her head and faced him calmly. Her voice was passionless. "Samuel, I am a Christian. She is my daughter. Of course I want her."

Samuel began to tremble and stepped back as if to protect himself from the coldness. "The *hell* you do! Well, let me tell you this, Mildred, from this minute she's *mine!* Do you hear? Don't you ever holler at her again. And never mind about taking care of her. *I'm* taking care of her. Just leave us alone! She's mine!"

He whirled around. Bobbie was standing in the doorway, the buttons of her coat done wrong, her knitted cap pulled almost over her eyes. Uncertainly she looked from one to the other, and then asked in a small voice, "Bobbie Daddy's little princess now?"

For a long time after the door slammed behind them, Mildred stood in the middle of the kitchen, aware, strangely of how clean it was. Then she threw back her head and welcomed a feeling of joy. The sound of her own laughter was a surprise.

With a lightness that was almost gaiety she filled the small dish with ice cream. Holding it in both hands, as if it were an offering, she went into the front room, placed it on a table and turned to her son. She lifted him in her arms, began to rock on her feet and nuzzled the top of his head with her face. Though she seemed to be looking through the stiffly starched lace curtains she did not see the brittle winter sunshine outside. Through a faint smile she muttered, "Of course, I can't let him take on *all* the care of her."

Quiet filled the room and she heard herself humming.

Softly she interrupted the song. "Sometimes I'll need to do things for her." After a long silence she whispered lightly, "After all, I didn't just *give* her away." The baby's head was warm and sweet to her cheek, and when he made a sound, love overwhelmed her. She held him at arm's length, drinking in his beauty, then clasped him to her and began to whirl around the room. Startled, the baby whimpered.

Mildred stopped her dance. Her voice was soft and tender, her face glowing. "Oh, did Mommie scare the baby? Mommie's sorry, darling. Mommie loves her sweet boy."

She moved to the straight chair beside the table and, settling the baby into the crook of her arm, she spooned a small amount of the melting ice cream between his moist pink lips. He moved the sweet taste around with his tongue and gently she scraped what escaped back into his mouth. She talked to him. Her voice became softer and higher and sweeter. She cooed. "Do you like this, my little angel? Mommie loves to give her baby good things...ooooh, such a sweet baby boy...."

Slowly she became aware of a tingling, working sensation in her drooping breasts. Her heart quickened with joy. She put the spoon in the bowl and pushed it away. Still looking into her baby's face, she fumbled with the buttons on the front of her dress, and pushed her brassiere strap off her shoulder. Lifting the limp breast out of her clothing, she pressed the baby to her, working the flaccid nipple into the soft mouth. Ecstacy filled her as the baby's tongue curled around it.

Her voice came faint and musical. "We're going to be fine now, my angel. Soon Mommie will be able to give you all the good sweet milk you need. And we won't need anyone else, will we, little darling?"

Her face bent to her child and she crooned. "Isn't that good?...yum, yum, yum...does my angel like that?" For a time she rocked gently back and forth in the chair, making little humming sounds. Then she murmured, "We didn't just *give* her away, did we, darling?"

Softly, sweetly, the sound of her voice went on.

"Nooooo...we wunna dus' *div* away nassy ol' sister, would we, little angel...we wunna dus' *div* her away...."

# The Day I Knew It Would be Okay

It was the summer she turned thirteen. One day she was all freckles and hurried, happy hugs and the next she had turned to legs and smart mouth. She hated school, me, her nose, her teachers, our house, her family. Nothing was right in her life. Her grades had gone from average to barely passing. She shot verbal shafts of insult when she bothered to speak at all. She yuck-hated the new dress I'd worked on so hard for which she herself had chosen the pattern and fabric. The occasional zit which appeared on her chin was absolute validation that her life had no meaning. Some days I wondered if mine did. Some days I doubted that the rest of her family would live through thirteen.

She sat beside me, silent and sullen, in the car. We were parked in a diagonal space in front of the neighborhood drug store waiting for her sister. I was as silent as she. No point in speaking, only to be put down by someone you must continually remind yourself you love. I'd stopped saying it to her, but repeated it often in my mind: "I love you, honey. But I hate the things you say and do."

We sat and stared straight ahead at the double glass doors

of the drug store. A bent old man in a faded blue jacket shuffled into our view. His clothes were clean, but they hung loosely on him, as if they'd been meant for the much larger man he probably once was. There was a pleasant look of anticipation on his face. His hair was freshly combed. I half expected some cynical comment from my right as he pushed the door open and went inside the drug store, but the silence ran on.

After a time, the old man reappeared at the door, and in his hand was a cone with a single dip of strawberry ice cream. We watched and it seemed to take him forever to get outside, be sure the door had closed behind him and shuffle a few feet away from it. There he paused and raised the cone to his mouth. He stuck out his pink tongue to lick it, but he pressed it too hard and the ice cream toppled from its precarious perch atop the cone and fell *splat* on the sidewalk.

Three boys running along the sidewalk saw it all and laughed and pointed. One of them jeered, "Too bad, Old Man. Better luck next time," and they all laughed again and ran on.

The old man stared helplessly at the pink mess on the sidewalk. I suppressed the need to help—to rush to him and offer to buy him another—to give him the change in my purse so he could buy another. But there was nothing I could do that wouldn't add to his humiliation. He began to wrap the napkin around the cone, looking around to see if anyone were watching. I cringed, hoping he wouldn't realize we were there inside the car. He didn't. Then, clutching the empty hidden cone to his chest, his shoulders drooping even lower, he walked slowly away.

From beside me I heard a little moan, "Oh, Mom..." I looked at her. Her gaze followed the old man. Her chin with its zit quivered and the freckled nose had turned pink. Tears filled her eyes.

And my own. Because in that moment, I knew everything was going to be okay.

# Showdown

They were lined up outside the post office, the same as every week day, some of them sitting on the old wooden bench, one or two leaning against the building.

They were the town's unoccupied men. That is, they weren't working because they had been laid off, or were on the night shift, or on disability. Or they were those who, for one reason or another, didn't hang around the pool hall across the street. A couple of them were teetotalers. And then, some men just don't like to be cooped up in a dark room in the daytime.

So what they did was gather outside the post office and wait for Addie Parsons to get the afternoon mail in the boxes. They called her the Postmistress although Addie claimed there wasn't any such a thing, that she was the Postmaster. Every day one of them would call her Postmistress Parsons and every day she would go into her speech, and they would laugh at her.

Other than trying to get Addie's goat, they talked and smoked (all except Lyle Harkins who chewed tobacco) and told old stories over again. They poked fun at everybody who passed, looking at each other with that we-may-not-be-much-but-we're-better'n-that-sorry-son-of-a-bitch expression on their faces.

The highlight of the day for the post office boys was when Olen Kappers came down the street on his daily jaunt to the pool hall. He never missed. It was a town joke that Olen shamed his church-going wife by getting half-drunk at the pool hall every day before supper, and the boys loved to torment him about it. They'd see him about the same time each day when he turned onto Main Street from Maple, his big old red bird dog, Duke, trotting along beside him. Duke was one of those long-legged, gangling bird dogs, so big that his head was higher than Olen's waist.

Olen always seemed to be thinking about something important, his eyes on the ground in front of him and his jaw set. Not in all the time the boys had been hassling him had he ever acted like he even heard them. As a matter of fact, he had never even looked at them. To the boys, that was intolerable. It somehow reflected on their position in the community. They would watch Olen all the way from Maple Street until he got about fifty yards from his destination, then they'd start hollering across the street. "Where you goin', Olen?" "Ain't you afraid the Old Lady'll find out where you are?" Or, "Now, you ain't gonna get a snootful, are you Olen?" Then they'd laugh with their nostrils distended and their lips raised so high their gums showed, and slap their thighs, and elbow each other.

The day in question started out to be nothing unusual for the boys. After they had gone inside and ribbed Addie, they all came out and took their positions and waited for something to happen. George Pugh needed a pack of cigarettes so he and Kenny Garrity walked down one block and across the street to the Safeway where they'd save a penny or two. George got his ciggies and Kenny got a bottle of pop and they came back and took their places.

One of the boys Lyle worked with on the night shift drove up and parked his new F150, the Harley Davidson edition, jet black and mean, at the curb and they all went out and looked it over. He opened the hood for them to show off the big five-point-four liter engine and they all walked around the truck, slapping it on the top and saying, "Yessir...." When the guy drove away, the engine rumbling deep in its belly, they gazed after him, and there was a period of silence during which each of them choked back seething jealousy of the shining new symbol of manhood and success.

Finally it got to be nearly time for Olen to appear. Once in a while somebody would glance up toward Maple Street, just checking.

Garrity, leaning against the building, raised his hand to his face, clamped down on the top of his nose with his forefinger and stuck his thumb inside. He was scraping away with his thumbnail when he happened to glance up the street in the other direction. He was so stunned by what he saw that for four or five seconds, he forgot to pick his nose and just stood there with his thumb up his nostril.

About two blocks away, coming down the sidewalk toward them, except on the other side of the street, was a woman. Even that far away Kenny could tell she was new in town, and what's more, she didn't look like any of the other women around there.

He took his thumb out of his nose and brushed it against the seat of his khakis. "For Christ' sake," he said, "who's that?"

"Who?" Lyle asked, then followed the direction of Kenny's gaze. "Oh! Well, fer...God, I don't know."

A silence followed while all of them stared. George mumbled, "Never saw her or anyone like her in this town before." He paused, then added, sarcastically, "And what's that? A dawg?"

It was. The lady who was the object of their interest was clicking along on high heels, proper as you please, with a little white dog dancing along in front of her on a leash.

Kenny said, "My, ain't she the prissy one!"

Lyle shot a stream of brown tobacco juice through his teeth into the gutter. "Look at that stupid dog. Shit! It'd fit in a pint fruit jar. W'y, that's one of them toy poodles. Why in hell would anyone want a dog like that? A dog like that ain't good for anything except to eat and yap and raise its leg." He smiled at his own witty remark and looked at the others for approval. But they all had their eyes fixed on the strange woman who, by that time, was passing the Safeway, about to cross the street to the sidewalk that ran in front of the pool hall.

"Wonder where she came from? Suppose she lives here in town?" somebody asked.

"Well, if she does, she just moved here. I'd sure as hell remember her if I'd ever seen her before." George noted to himself that she was tall and thin, and wore a navy blue suit. Women around there didn't wear suits. She had on high heels and a hat, of all things. She kept her eyes straight ahead and held tightly to the leash.

"Hey," said Kenny, "I'll bet she's the new librarian over at the school. They haven't had one since Miss Kurtlie died, but I heard the school board was about to hire somebody."

"You must be right. Nobody but a school teacher would dress like that," Lyle observed. He got grunts of agreement from the group.

"Where do you suppose she thinks she's goin'—to the pool hall?" Garrity asked, and they all sniggered. Their eyes followed her as she proceeded along the street, taking little short steps and wiggling her hind end, while holding the top part of herself stiff as a stick. He couldn't tell for sure, because of the suit jacket, but Kenny figured she probably had big tits. Lots of women with big tits walked that way.

"The only place that woman would be goin' is to JoAnne's." Lyle was referring to JoAnne's Hairdressing Salon which was three doors past the pool hall, toward Maple Street.

"I don't think so, Lyle," George cracked. "Don't look to me like she'd take that hat off for nobody. Maybe it just grows there." He chuckled.

They watched her while everybody tried to think of something funny to say. Then Garrity, who had been sitting on the wooden bench, happened to glance up toward Maple Street. He jumped to his feet.

"Oh, shit!" he hissed. "Here comes Olen and Duke. Jesus!

What's going to happen when they meet the lady and the poodle?"

Excitement lit up his face and he looked at his cronies. They were all standing at attention. In their eyes was the same kind of anticipation seen at a boxing match when a fighter goes in for the kill.

George licked his lips.

Lyle whirled around, put his forehead against the stucco of the Post Office and slapped the wall beside his head. "W'y Duke'll eat that poodle alive!" he snorted.

George pushed his sweat-stained Caterpillar cap back, revealing a pale forehead that didn't match the rest of his sun-reddened face. Grinning, he hooked his thumbs in his belt loops and, thrusting out his pelvis, rocked forward on his feet, then back, and glanced around at the rest of the group. "This is goin' to be the best show since Sheriff Long ran his car through the window of LaMode's Dress Shoppe."

The boys moved out and lined up along the curb. Their eyes darted from the lady with the poodle to Olen and Duke, like they were watching a tennis match. Olen strode along, head down, as always. He was wearing clean striped overalls and a starched and ironed blue chambray shirt. His wife may not have been able to keep him from going to the pool hall, but she could keep him from going to the pool hall dirty, and she figured if he couldn't be Godly, at least he could be clean. The sun shone off his bald head and lit up the white hair that grew thick at the sides and back. Ol' Duke loped along beside him, bumping Olen's elbow once in a while with his big, hard head.

Olen and Duke were getting closer to the lady and the poodle. The boys on the curb began to lean forward. They'd look at Olen, then at the lady with the navy blue purse and matching pumps, and try to judge how long it would be before the inevitable happened.

"Jesus! Ain't they ever goin' to look up?" George whispered.

He no sooner got the words out of his mouth than the woman raised her eyes and saw Olen and Duke. She stopped dead, jerking at the poodle's leash. The little ball of fluff abruptly changed ends and looked up at his mistress with his head cocked to one side. She drew in the leash, pulling the dog closer to her. She seemed undecided about what to do. After a few seconds, she took another step or two, hesitated and stopped again.

About that time Olen raised his head and saw her. Automatically he put his hand on Duke's head to calm him. Duke had seen the poodle, of course, and suddenly he appeared to weigh another fifty pounds as his thick, long, red coat puffed out along his spine.

"Woof," he said softly.

"Easy, Duke, easy." Olen soothed the dog while he sized up the situation. He could feel the big bird dog's flesh rippling nervously under his hand. "Easy boy, easy there." Then, warily, he resumed his walk toward the pool hall, which, by that time, the lady had passed.

That was when the poodle saw Ol' Duke and started the worst noise since the Pork Festival Parade with the Drum and Bugle Corp just behind the bagpipes. "YAP-yap-yap-yap-yap, YAP-yap-yap-yap-yap!"

The yapping activated the lady's protective instincts. In one wild motion, she swooped down and gathered up the hysterical poodle and hugged the bundle of jerking yelps and yips to her, turned away slightly, and looked like she might scream. Then she got hold of herself. Sticking her nose in the air as if there was no one in the world but her and the poodle that she cuddled to her, she resumed her prissy walk toward Olen and Duke, her high heels clacking on the sidewalk to add to the ear-splitting yapping of the dog.

Olen, his hand still quieting Duke who quivered in a sort of a "point," stared with disbelief at the snooty lady walking toward him carrying her silly dog in her arms. For a second he didn't seem to know what to do. Then his eyes narrowed, and the boys across the street could see that he had come to a decision.

Olen puckered his mouth in at the corners and his nose went into the air, just like the lady's, and with a flourish that began with a graceful outward lift of both arms, his fingers extended in a tea-cup attitude, he bent down and picked up Ol' Duke. With one arm under his dog's haunches and the other under his chest, he clasped the huge animal to his breast. In splendid dignity, he resumed his journey, twisting his butt when he walked just as the lady approaching him was doing.

Poor Ol' Duke. Humiliation made his mournful face even longer. The way Olen was holding him, his tail was tucked under him, and his front legs crossed over his back legs, and still they bounced off of Olen's knees with every step. He turned his head and looked up at Olen, a plea for mercy in his sad eyes.

Every one of the boys in front of the Post Office held his breath. The players in the drama got closer and closer. It looked like they were going to walk right smack into one another. Then, when they were no more than two steps apart, Olen lowered his head in a gesture of noble courtesy and took one step back and one to the right, never missing a beat, and they passed.

Just for an instant, Ol' Duke forgot his part and stretched his big head out to sniff at the yapping poodle, rooting his nose down between the lady's arm and the dog, to try to get it in just the right spot to answer his instinctive question. The lady withered him with her glance then snapped her head around and continued clacking down the street, as if the whole degrading episode had never happened.

Across the street all eyes were fixed on Olen and all mouths hung open. In grudging but real admiration, the boys watched as Olen neared the open pool hall door. There he put Ol' Duke down, patted him on the rump to send him inside, and turned around. The set of his head and the cool cast of his eye as he stood facing Main Street left no doubt about who was in charge of the moment. His primacy was absolute.

Slowly, majestically, he bowed, bringing his hands together in front of him, one over the other, like the maestro of a great orchestra, except he didn't have a baton. He held the pose, as if he were waiting for something.

For a moment there was silence on Main Street while the boys at the Post Office tried to figure out what was expected of them. Then Lyle began to clap his hands, slowly at first, then faster, and all the others joined in. Addie Parsons stepped out of the Post Office, smiling and clapping. George Pugh put his thumb and forefinger in his mouth and whistled. From the dark interior of the pool hall behind Olen came more applause.

The clapping went on and on until people started sticking their heads out of stores and coming out on the sidewalk to see what was going on. When they figured out that the boys at the Post Office were clapping for Olen Kappers, bent over there in the doorway of the pool hall, they clapped, too. The message was working its way along Main Street, passing from person to person and as each one heard it the applause got louder. Pretty soon people all up and down the street were clapping and hollering and whistling.

Olen's timing was perfect. At exactly the right moment, before the noise began to die down, he raised himself to his full height and assumed an attitude of haughty superiority. Regally he turned, and head high, back straight above the baggy seat of his striped overalls, Olen Kappers entered the pool hall and for the first time in his life, got quietly and contentedly drunk on free beer.

# A Well-Arranged Life

Liz is a mile and a half into her run, her customized running shoes flupping along the concrete walkway that edges the small manmade urban lake. When she must move to the right, uncomfortably close to the water, to make way for a couple who do not acknowledge her courtesy, her irritation resurfaces. She had almost forgotten the reason for it in the thought-damping rhythm of running.

Flup. Flup. Flup.

The call from her brother has upset her. The result of it will be an interruption of her well-arranged life. She knows the dangers inherent in interruption. Knows that one fosters another, and, if they're tolerated, disorder is inevitable.

Nothing Ted could have said would have persuaded her to interrupt the discipline of her life except what he did say. That they must talk about Mother. When she suggested that they could talk on the telephone, Ted had become uncharacteristically firm. Ted is never firm. "No. I want you to come to St. Louis," he had said in his unpracticed assertiveness. But he refused to tell her what it was that he felt must be discussed in person. Money, perhaps, she thinks. Well, she can afford to contribute more. Though she is not well-to-do, thanks to good financial planning, money is no particular problem. Ted has always been so exasperatingly embarrassed to ask.

Her disapproval of Ted's aversion to conflict is strong. She believes it is that weakness that has resulted in the indulgent lifestyle that he allows himself and his family. That was among the arguments for her leaving St. Louis, three years ago. Another was Ted's faintly amused tolerance of, and her mother's refusal to recognize as important, the life that Liz had chosen to make for herself. Their unreasonable views on the subject had become a constant undercurrent, as present as an unwelcome relative, at all the family gatherings.

So Liz is satisfied that her—estrangement is too strong a word, she thinks—her *separation* from them is a good thing. That there had been no sense of crisis when she had announced that she was moving to the coast, was evidence of the rightness of her decision. She had, of course, asked her mother to come with her, and felt only the briefest flare of hurt (resentment) when she had chosen to stay with Ted in St. Louis. It was only natural, Liz told herself, that her mother would want to be near her grandchildren. Liz denies that she is now grateful, but admits that living alone is essential to her disciplined life, and that, in turn, is essential to her emotional well-being. She has come to terms with it and no longer feels any guilt that her mother lives fulltime with Ted. He seems not to mind.

Liz wonders how a brother and sister can be so different. Perhaps because she is so much older. She was twelve, and already clearly blessed with her mother's tall and spare, strong and resilient body, when Ted made his plump little appearance. From the first it was obvious that he had inherited his father's obesity. Just ten months after Ted squawled his way into the world from their mother's contracting womb, their father quietly and quickly made his way out, a victim of the uncontrolled contractions of his over-taxed heart. Liz had been quite old enough to see clearly the tragedy of her 42-year-old father's death and had, at thirteen, put into practice habits of diet and exercise that would enhance her natural health and assure her a lifespan at least double his. She had never let up. Nor will I, she thinks.

Flup. Flup. Flup.

She looks at her legs as she runs. Slender, muscular, hard. Not a gram of extra flesh. She glories in the vanity her superb body entitles her to. It is more attractive, and certainly healthier, than those of co-workers twenty years her junior. She raises her head and draws in the summer-warm air. She feels her breath deep in her lungs and the steady strong beat of her steady, strong heart. Sometimes, as now, Liz feels she will live forever.

Flup. Flup.

She wipes perspiration from her neck with her wrist band. She will have to go to St. Louis, of course. But she will make the trip short. She will fly there tomorrow, spend the following day with her mother, Ted, Grace, and the children, like a dutiful daughter/sister, and fly back the third day. Even that is too long, Liz thinks. She avoids traveling. Traveling makes sticking to diet and exercise schedules extremely difficult. Still, she can run tomorrow very early, before she leaves, and again the next day in St. Louis. But she is afraid she cannot work it in on the third day. Connections are bad. Uneasiness lowers over her as she thinks about missing her run.

Ted is waiting, smiling, when Liz comes down the ramp. He is as fat as ever. He waddles toward her, his thighs working his trousers into his crotch. Liz swallows disgust. She also swallows an unexpected rush of love, and pity, and a small fear for him.

Ted asks about luggage and she tells him she has brought only a carry-on, so, no, they won't need to go to the baggage claim. She hands the bag to him. In it are tailored slacks and pullovers. (Liz is wearing tailored slacks and a pullover. She wears these most of the time. Other women envy her tight buttocks and flat stomach.) Also in the bag are specially formulated vitamins and her just broken-in running shoes. When they reach the car, she checks to be sure Ted still has the bag. She would hate losing her running shoes.

She and Ted find little to talk about on the way to his house. Her job is going well. He tells her that Grace is fine. Theodore has discovered computers and Mary Jane has discovered boys.

"And Mother?"

Ted pauses before he answers her, and there is an instant when she is afraid her mother is ill. "She's strong," he says. "Her doctor...remember old Doctor Whitty?...he listens to her heart and lungs and takes blood for testing regularly, and he says she's in fine shape." Liz is relieved.

When the car stops at the maple-shaded curb, Liz sees her mother standing in the open door and acknowledges a moment of pride. Her mother is still a handsome woman. Still tall and spare, strong and resilient. Her hair is white but thick and has been nicely styled. She wears a flattering rose-colored dress. She is smiling.

Liz mounts the steps and says, "Hello, Mother." She wraps her arms around her and is surprised, almost dismayed, at her own strong emotion.

Her mother's voice is the same. "My dear," she says, "it is wonderful to see you. Here, let me look at you." She holds Liz at arm's length. "My dear, you are the picture of your mother."

Liz giggles at her mother's unexpected joke, and she thinks that living with Ted's family must agree with her. She places her arm around the shoulders that are still as tall and straight as her own, and says, "Let's go inside."

In the hallway, they hesitate and her mother folds and refolds her hands in front of her. Then she says, "Come in and sit down, darling, and tell me all about yourself." She opens a door and motions Liz in. They are in a storeroom.

Ted appears in the doorway of the room with Liz's bag in his hand. With his free hand he takes his mother's elbow and turns her. "No, Mother," he says gently, "the living room is this way."

Liz is packing. In a few minutes Ted will come to her room to pick her up and take her to the airport.

She is trying to decide whether she should be angry with him for not preparing her. He said, when they sat down last night to talk, that he had felt she should see for herself. He said that he didn't think she would have accepted their mother's condition on his word. She decides she can't be angry with him. She would not have accepted it.

Acceptance has come with pain. She remembers seeing her mother spill food down the lovely rose dress and leave it, unnoticed. She remembers being called by her mother's dead sister's name, and by the name of a distant cousin, and with her mother's eyes searching hers frantically, by no name at all. She remembers waking in the night to find a wraith with wild white hair in her room and watching it go to the closet and open the door. She remembers that her heart broke when Grace appeared, took the wraith's arm and said to Liz, "She's looking for the bathroom." Liz wonders if her mother wet herself at the back yard barbecue the day before because she couldn't remember where the bathroom was, or because she wasn't aware she was doing it. She remembers that Ted was embarrassed when he told her that their mother was mean and petulant and that she pinched his children if they got too close to her. Liz remembers opening her mouth to call him a liar, and that she had cried, instead.

She wipes new tears from her face. She folds a gray pull-over and places it in the carry-on. Then she reaches for her running shoes.

She stops. She is holding one shoe in each hand and is very still. For a time she stares at the shoes, then she raises her eyes to see herself in the dressing table mirror across the room. She sees a body perfectly maintained. It is tall and spare, strong and resilient.

She walks to the corner of the room where there is a small wicker trash basket. She drops one shoe, and then the other, into the basket.

Flup. Flup.

# Billy and Benjamin Too

The two boys sat on the top rail of the rustic fence between the vacation cabin and the lake. The sun shone, glinting off their hair and blinking off the water. It was deep summer and the lake was low and still.

The mother, inside the cabin, glanced up from her book and stared across her quietly snoring husband stretched out in the recliner. She watched the boy and thought about him and hoped, again, that he would come out of this whatever it was. It had been two years, for goodness' sake. Her heart ached for him and for the loss of his brother. What was it that Billy missed so much? A twin brother to love? Or a twin brother to control or maybe even to hurt? She shook the thought out of her head.

Benjamin Too had been the sweet one of the twins and she had to constantly suppress the wish that things had worked out the other way around. It was her guilty secret and it ate at her. God had taken her sweet child and left her with Billy. Billy was hard to love. Sometimes she believed that he didn't want to be loved. Secretly she acknowledged that she was sometimes afraid of her son. Just last week they'd had to give away the puppy they'd bought for him in the hope it would help him "adjust." Billy's daddy had responded to the yelping puppy only to find a giggling Billy clamping clothespins onto the poor creature's testicles.

Was it from the first that they'd seen the difference in the two boys? It had been obvious in the delivery room that Billy would be the strong twin; he was bigger, and beautiful, his eyes large and knowing, his hair thick and jet black. Four minutes later Benjamin Too had appeared, small, thin, with a swirl of mouse-brown hair. They'd given the boys the family names, William for the big beautiful baby who immediately became Billy; Benjamin II for the smaller twin. When people came to see them, they'd shown the big beautiful baby first, and then said, "And Benjamin, too." The play on words stuck. Now Benjamin Too was gone. And they were left with Billy. Billy: hard to love.

There was a sound from the bedroom and the mother was instantly alert. It was Baby, making a peaceful noise in her sleep. The mother's face softened. She was smiling as she turned back to her book.

If she'd been outside, closer to the boy sitting on the fence, she'd have heard him talking. "Come on, Benjamin Too. You never want to do anything. You're such a squeeb."

"Am not."

"You are so. Even before, you never wanted to do anything that was fun. You weren't any fun, ever."

"I'm fun," Benjamin Too said softly. "We have fun, Billy. remember when we found the boat and spent the whole day rowing all over the lake? Wasn't that fun?"

Billy drew in a breath and said, "Yeah. I guess so. But most of the time there's nothin' to do. This summer's never gonna be over. And when it is, I have to go back to school and that's no fun, neither. The other kids don't like me. None of 'em do. And I hate them."

Benjamin Too squirmed inside his cloud. Billy watched. That stupid cloud. Billy didn't know what it was made of because it was always changing. Sometimes it was just gold dust, and sometimes just fog, but sometimes it had solid things in it that moved around and other times it wiggled like Jell-O. If it wasn't for that stupid cloud, he'd have Benjamin Too back just like before. A couple of times he'd tried to get hold of it and tear it off, but it was like his hands closed on nothing. And Benjamin Too didn't seem to think it was important. He was no help at all.

"I'll be there, Billy, when you go back to school."

"Oh, sure. When you want to be. But not all the time. Not when *I* want you to be around."

"I'll try, Billy. but I can't be there just any old time. It doesn't work that way." He paused and mumbled, "I think it's because I'm afraid you don't want me. Sometimes you act mad."

"It's because when you died and then you undied, I thought it would be the same as always. But it's not."

"Would you like it better if I was still dead, Billy?"

Billy jerked to attention. "Stop it. Damn you, Benjamin Too, you stop it!"

Benjamin Too smiled and said, his voice soft and sweet. "Okay, Billy, I was just teasin'." He picked at a scab on his knee. When he touched it, it disintegrated into a puff of dust. He raised his head and watched the dust blow away, leaving a little blank trail behind it in his cloud.

He spoke then, still softly, and carefully, like he had to say what he had to say but didn't want to, "You know, Billy... before? Sometimes what you thought was fun...wasn't very nice."

Billy sulked. "Who cares about 'nice'?"

Benjamin Too's voice got even quieter, so quiet Billy could hardly hear it—but he didn't need to hear it to know what his brother was saying. Benjamin Too said, "You made me help you do bad things."

Billy screwed up his mouth and rolled his eyes. "I didn't do no such a thing. You could always say you didn't want to." He knew very well that his twin had said that many times, and that mostly Benjamin Too had refused him, but then when he got so mad that he hit things hard and made his fists bleed, and he made that growling, screaming noise deep in his throat, Benjamin Too would give in and do whatever Billy wanted. Billy was quiet, thinking about that, then he said, "Okay. It's your turn to say what we can do now for fun. Mom's reading, like always, and Dad's asleep in the recliner, like always. Baby's down for her nap—like I wish she was always. We can do anything we want to."

Benjamin Too jumped down off the rail and said, "Let's go to the water." He smiled his beautiful smile. That smile was so bright and shiny through Benjamin Too's little cloud that it kinda scared Billy. In two years since his brother died then undied, Billy had got used to the fact that the new Benjamin Too would come and go, and that he was in that dumb cloud, but he just couldn't get used to that smile. It was—Billy thought of the word 'beautiful'—but he also thought of the word 'weird' and then, 'unnatural.' Sometimes it gave Billy a shiver, the same kind of a shiver he got when he watched his "Frankenstein's Monster" video. He couldn't decide if it was the nicest thing he ever saw, or just the weirdest.

Benjamin Too was hopping down the long beach that got browner and muddier the closer they got to the water. He seemed happy, and Billy liked that. He hated being afraid Benjamin Too would go away. That was the worst thing, when Benjamin Too was there and then he wasn't, and Billy didn't know how to get him back. When that happened, Billy felt like he was out in space, just floating around like a kite with a busted string, with no way to get back to earth. When that happened, he felt like he'd lost control, and that was bad. Very bad. It made Billy crazy.

He didn't know exactly if the boy in the thin, wiggly cloud who ran down the beach in front of him was a real boy or what, so he didn't know if Benjamin Too could die again, and if he did, if he could come back again. What he was pretty sure about was that if Benjamin Too wanted to fade away to nothing, he could. It made Billy mad that Benjamin Too could do that. And it scared him. He got mad again, then, because he hated it when he was scared of something. Of anything.

Benjamin Too stopped suddenly and looked back at Billy and smiled that smile. There were rays of that smile sticking way out of his cloud. Even several feet away, Billy thought he could feel it. Benjamin Too said, "Let's play in the mud—we'll squeeze it through our toes."

Billy sighed. "Sheez, Benjamin Too, that's kid stuff. Think of something else."

Benjamin Too turned and walked toward the water again, slowly. "I can't think of anything," he muttered.

Billy said, "Dad's rifle's in the closet. We could shoot birds."

Benjamin Too's answer was quick. "No! I don't want to. Don't make me."

Billy thought it over. "Okay. Hey," he lowered his voice and giggled, "let's sneak into the cabin and see if Baby's asleep and then stick her with one of those pins that Mom keeps in the tray on top of the chest. Baby'll scream and Mom will come running like a crazy woman. We'll hide in the closet. Remember when we pinched Baby and Mom ran so fast she stumbled over the rocking chair and took all the skin off her knee?" He was laughing.

"We can't do that Billy. Baby's just a...baby. Nobody hurts babies."

"Hell, Benjamin Too, she's not a baby anymore. She's a whole year old and she can walk. And she's got teeth."

"You ought not to say 'hell.' Baby can't eat by herself, except for Cheerios off her high chair tray, and she can't dress herself, or take a bath by herself or anything. She's still a baby, even if she can walk."

Billy dropped the idea. Benjamin Too was beginning to sound a little bit upset. That worried Billy but having Benjamin Too take up for Baby made him mad. Why did everybody have to try to protect Baby all the time? He said, "Yeah, you're right. She *is* a baby. That's why they make such a fuss over her all the time. That's why they don't pay any attention to me. That and you and your stupid loo-kem-ia or whatever it was. How come you had to die? That was a mean thing you did to me. You did it on purpose! We had things goin' real good for us. Everything was working out okay. Then you had to go and die." He stopped, pulled at the neck of his tee shirt and went on, "So then they thought the only thing to do was have another kid. So now they've got another kid and, like, I'm nothin'. It's Baby this, Baby that." He twisted and simpered, "'Oh, honey, isn't she cute. Oh, look at her. Look at that curly hair. Look at those sweet little fingers.' Makes me want to puke."

Benjamin too didn't say anything for a minute. "Baby's okay. And she really is kinda cute."

"She is not! And it's all your fault she was ever born. I hate you for dying. You messed up everthing."

Benjamin Too stared at the brown mud at his feet. "I'm sorry, Billy. I didn't mean to, honest. I tried not to die—I did what the doctors said, but it just didn't work. It made me feel so sick, made me puke up my insides, but I didn't want to leave you, Billy." He paused. "Well, sometimes I did, but mostly I didn't. Honest, Billy, I tried not to die."

"You're a liar."

"I am not, Billy. You're my brother. I never wanted to die and leave you."

"You coulda' stayed if you wanted to."

Benjamin Too's face didn't get set hard very often, and when it did, it didn't last long. But it got set then. "I can leave right now, Billy, and never come back," he said.

Billy sucked in his breath and snapped, "No! Don't leave me. You're all I got now. Nobody cares about me. There's nobody to have fun with. Even if there's lots of stuff you can't do, you're better'n nobody." There was panic in Billy's black eyes. He began to plead. "Don't go, Benjamin Too. Don't go. Okay? We'll do whatever you want. Come on, let's squirt mud with our feet."

"Okay." Benjamin Too smiled and Billy's breath came easier. They took off running toward the water, throwing off their shoes as they ran.

It was fun, squishing mud, and they worked on a technique for squirting the thin, brown stuff through their toes, and controlling the direction of the squirt, but they didn't get very good at it. Most of the time they missed each other, but they hit their marks often enough that Billy's clothes were ruined.

"How come dirt don't stick to you, Benjamin Too?"

"How should I know? I'm just here. Just waitin' around, kinda."

"For what?"

"I don't know. It's like there's something I forgot to do, but it seems like if I think about it hard enough I will remember it. Then I get to feelin' like if I do whatever it is, then I won't be able to stay here with you, Billy. So I don't try too hard to remember. Maybe I won't ever remember. That would be okay. I'd rather play in the mud with you."

Billy felt a shudder in his stomach. What was Benjamin Too talking about?...that if he did what he was supposed to do, maybe he couldn't stay? Billy was afraid of being alone. And it was true that he didn't have anybody but his brother. He'd lost his mother and dad when Benjamin Too died. They just sorta weren't there anymore. And then one day he'd heard his mom on the phone to his grandma saying they'd decided to have a baby, and there was a silence and she had said, "I guess so—I guess to take the place of Benjamin Too." And when Baby was born, his parents went even further away. They were there but they weren't. They saw he had food and clothes and school supplies and they made him brush his teeth, but he wasn't sure they ever saw him. It felt like they looked all the way through him. Just like he could see all the way through Benjamin Too when Benjamin Too did that hateful thing of fading away.

Billy didn't fully understand just what had happened that night a few weeks after Benjamin Too died, and Billy was alone in his bed, and there was no world. With his twin gone, Billy didn't have a world. He didn't have anything. Nothing. And then, just like it used to be, he had felt Benjamin Too climbing into his bunk. He was warm, but when Billy pushed at him, he couldn't feel anything except that warmth. There was a Benjamin Too-shaped lump under the covers but when he raised the covers and looked, at first he couldn't see anything at all. Then he could see something sorta like fog; like seeing your breath on a cold morning. It was scary, but suddenly a Benjamin Too formed inside the fog and Billy had never been so happy.

The next few nights Benjamin Too had come and they had talked and talked. Billy was naturally curious about a lot of things, and asked Benjamin Too if he would grow along with Billy. Benjamin Too didn't know but he thought he could. And Billy asked him how he worked. "Do you eat and drink water?"

"I don't know. I don't ever get hungry. Or thirsty. Anyway, I don't know what would happen to stuff after I ate it or drank it."

"Can you pee?"

"I don't think so. I don't feel like I need to pee. You know how that feels, when it kinda stretches your insides and if you don't go to the bathroom pretty soon, then it really hurts? I don't get that...y'know...that hurt place."

"Can you poop?"

"No. But...."

"But what?"

"Well, I can..." Benjamin Too squirmed and lowered his eyes, "...I can pass gas."

"You can fart!" Billy was delighted. "Do it."

"I don't know if I can do it just any old time I want to."

"Oh, man. Come on. Fart!"

Benjamin Too wiggled inside his cloud. That went on for a couple of minutes. Then he relaxed and said, "There."

"I didn't hear anything."

"Well, I guess I can't make a noise."

"Oh, Benjamin Too, you can't fart. You're just kiddin' me. Hell with you. You're a creep." Billy turned away in disgust, then suddenly he got still. "Oh, sheez! Benjamin Too! Phew. Man, that stinks." But he laughed aloud. It was wonderful that the weird Benjamin Too that he had now could fart. If he could fart just like a real boy, it made him less likely to just fade away. "That was cool, Benjamin Too. Thanks. Thanks a lot."

"You're welcome."

Billy had felt very close to his brother at that moment.

Carefully, and slowly so as not to cause any kind of a reaction, he had put his arm around his brother. It worked. Benjamin Too didn't go away.

But now, nearly two years after Benjamin Too died and then undied, Billy still wasn't sure just what to do and what not to do to keep things just like they were. He didn't want to screw up and lose this Benjamin Too like he lost the first one. Billy would be alone, and there wouldn't be anybody to do what he wanted them to do. He had to have his brother even in that stupid cloud.

They'd got tired of squirting mud. Billy found a big log nearby and sat on it. Benjamin Too came and sat beside him, close enough that Billy could feel his cloud. Billy looked out across the water. He was quiet. Benjamin Too was always quiet. Billy thought about putting his hand on his brother's leg, but he was a little bit afraid of that, too. Finally he worked up his nerve and tried it. Benjamin Too looked at him and smiled that weird, beautiful smile and then he giggled. Billy gave his twin's thigh a slap. Benjamin Too just kept on grinning and giggling, and nothing else happened. It made Billy feel good.

Frogs croaked and birds sang and somewhere far off a dog barked. And Billy felt good.

And it took only about two minutes for him to forget and become the tortured Billy again. So, when he saw the frog, he put his foot out and mashed it into the mud.

"Don't Billy. He'll die!"

"Who cares? It's just a frog."

Benjamin Too reached out of his cloud and grabbed Billy's tee shirt and began to pull. "Stop it. Stop it, Billy."

Something snapped in Billy when Benjamin Too pulled at his shirt. He whirled. "Get your hands off of me, you creep." He yanked his shirt away and reached down into the mud and closed his hand around the frog. With a grunt, he hurled it with all his might against a rock. The frog flopped once and lay still. Billy's eyes were black and cold, and then he began to smile and slowly, slowly nod his head up and down, up and down.

After a moment, he looked at his brother. But Benjamin Too was already half gone. Faded to nearly nothing inside his little cloud. Billy screamed, "No! No, no. Don't go Benjamin Too. Come back." And then, in desperation, "I love you, Benjamin Too. You're my brother. I need you."

Just as slowly as Benjamin Too had faded away, he reappeared. Billy watched, his face white and tight, his fists clinching at his sides. When he was sure Benjamin Too was there again, tears filled his eyes. Benjamin Too reached out his hand then, but Billy was angry at being made to cry and he moved away. "Don't."

Benjamin Too's feelings were hurt but he didn't want to make Billy angry again so soon. He turned and walked slowly up the slope toward the cabin. Then he heard Billy running after him. "I didn't mean for you not to touch me, Benjamin Too. Honest. I didn't mean it."

Benjamin Too had heard it all before. He'd spent the better part of his six years on earth and the two after he died, being pushed around, forced into doing things he knew he ought not to do, then watching as Billy pretended to be sorry. Sometimes Benjamin Too had even taken the punishment when he didn't do anything bad. And here he was, letting Billy do it to him again. He ought to just disappear, once and for all. He knew he ought to. That would serve Billy right. He didn't know why he didn't. Yes, he did. Sort of. He knew he was here to do something and he couldn't go away for good until it was done. Whatever it was. And inside that feeling was one that told him that if he went away, Billy might do something awful. Benjamin Too knew it. So then he wondered how long he was supposed to hang around. Sheez, it could be all of Billy's life, and Benjamin Too wasn't sure he even wanted to do that. He remembered that real life wasn't all that great. Sometimes you had to do homework and sometimes you got cut or hit and it hurt, and sometimes you got sick and that was awful.

"Come on!"

"No."

Billy walked beside Benjamin Too, but he was very quiet.

After a while, he turned to him and, all innocent and sweet, said, "What's the matter, Benjamin Too?"

"You're mean, Billy."

"*You're* the mean one, Benjamin Too. You won't do anything I want to do. First you die on me, then you come back in that funny little ol' cloud thing and I think everything's okay, then you won't do anything I want to do."

"You were mean, even before. You were mean to me, sometimes, and you hurt the puppy so bad that Dad took it away. And now you want to be mean to Baby."

Billy was disgusted. "It's not mean to want to have a little fun. It's just natural." His breath huffed out suddenly and he said, "Well, if you don't want to have fun, then just stay down here. Jis' go back down there and sit on the dumb rock and see if I care. I can have fun by myself. You know it don't hurt Baby to get stuck with a little ol' pin, or get pinched a little bit. Just a little bitty red spot and it goes away in no time. Nobody would ever know we did anything."

Benjamin Too had gone back to the rock and climbed up. He was quiet for a minute, then like he was working up nerve, he said, "No Billy. If you do that I'll...I'll...."

Billy stopped. He clinched his fists at his sides. "No, Benjamin Too. No...no...don't do that. The last time I didn't know where to find you and you stayed away and stayed away." But as he watched, Benjamin Too began to fade. He got dimmer and dimmer inside his cloud. Billy reached out slowly and put his hand into the cloud. "No, Benjamin Too. I won't do it. Don't go."

Then all at once, he felt fingers in his and he gave a little tug and there was his brother. He had his cloud the same as always, but that was okay. It was just part of the Benjamin Too that Billy had now. This twin was better than nothing. And that's what he had without Benjamin Too. Nothin'. Nothin'. He felt the stupid tears starting again.

Billy's insides felt empty. Not hungry. Well, maybe hungry for something he couldn't name. Maybe he just wanted his old life back. When Benjamin Too, the *first* Benjamin Too, was there, Billy had always been the boss. He'd always been able to make his brother do what he wanted, and most of the time he still could. But now, with the old Benjamin Too dead, when the new Benjamin Too made up his mind to fade away, it scared the poop out of Billy. Because Benjamin Too could do it. Benjamin Too had found a way to be the boss. Billy didn't like that. Not at all. And he was caught in a trap. Do what Benjamin Too wanted, or he could just fade away.

And there were the times when Benjamin Too just didn't show up. Some mornings when Billy woke, Benjamin Too wasn't there. And Billy didn't know how to call him. Didn't know how to make him just suddenly *be* there. Once or twice Billy had been really mad—the Billy kind of mad that made him stomp and hit things and bang his head against the wall and make that scream that was more of a grunt, or a growl, down deep in his throat, because Benjamin Too wasn't there when he wanted him. Sometimes he even hated Benjamin Too. Even if the new Benjamin Too was all he had now. He wanted his twin to be beside him *all* the time, and he wanted him to do what he wanted.

And when Benjamin Too wouldn't, then Billy got mad. The Billy kind of mad.

One morning he had gone down to the water because Benjamin Too just didn't show up. Wasn't there when Billy woke up, and an hour later hadn't shown up. Billy was half lonely and half mad. He sat on the rock for a while, but he was restless so he went back up to the cabin. His mom was reading her book—that's what his mom did when she wasn't doing something for Baby or holding Baby or just cooing like a fool at Baby. His dad was in the recliner. Billy couldn't remember that his dad slept so much before the first Benjamin Too died. Nowadays his mom and dad hardly ever talked to each other. Or to Billy. Just to Baby. About all they ever said to each other and to him was 'please' and 'thank you.' Billy hadn't ever thought how those words could sound bad.

So that day when he went in the back door to get a drink of water and heard them talking, he stopped and listened. "Strange boy. Yeah. He isn't the kid he was before. He was always smart and funny, even though he was pretty hard to handle. Now he isn't happy. He isn't even *here,* if you know what I mean. He spends too much time alone in his room. And then there's that weird talking. Talking to his imaginary friend."

His mom said, "The psychologist says that's okay. It's 'compensatory,' she says. He's compensating for losing Benjamin Too."

"I know what she says. It just gives me the creeps, that's all."

His mom's voice was low. "I used to like to hug the boys, but now he's just so offish. He acts like he would be upset if I put my hands on him. So I guess I'm happy that I've got Baby to take care of. It's like Billy doesn't want to be taken care of." She was quiet for a moment and then she said, "I guess I have to come to grips with something...I don't like Billy right now."

Billy held his breath, waiting for his dad to take up for him, but his dad didn't say anything. Nothing. He wanted to hurt his dad. Hurt him bad. His shoulders pulled up and twisted. He wanted to hurt his mom, too. It would feel so good to hit her. Hit her with his fist in her nasty mouth.

"It's just that Baby is the sweetest child. She's like Benjamin Too was. She's never angry, she never cries for things. You never have to worry about her, just do the ordinary things you do for a baby. She's so happy. She smiles and coos and laughs all the time. She's everything you want your child to be." She was quiet. "And Billy's everything I never wanted for a son." She sighed. "I'm sorry. I know that's wrong. I know that's not a normal feeling for a mother to have about her child, but it's true. If he'd just behave like a normal boy, running around, making noise, grabbing cookies, even getting in trouble, I could handle that." Her voice got small. "But he's...Billy is...different. Now. He didn't used to be...different, did he?"

The silence before his dad spoke was just an instant too long. Then he said, "No. No. Our twins were normal boys. Noisy and a little wild and always doing something you didn't expect. Benjamin Too was a nice little boy—we always knew that—and Billy was the troublemaker. But it was a good balance. Billy was wild, but Benjamin Too calmed him down. Now Billy isn't exactly wild any more. Except when he has those—*incidents*."

"You mean his temper tantrums. Call them what they are."

"The shrink doesn't call them temper tantrums."

"I know that. But that's what they are. He's—he's violent. He might hurt himself."

His dad didn't say anything for a time and Billy could barely hear him when he spoke. "There's something about Billy now. Something that makes me feel strange." There was another silence and then his dad said, "Kinda' afraid. Of him. Or for him. Oh, I don't know." He drew in a long breath and Billy heard the chair squeak as he got out of it. He asked, "Want a glass a tea?"

Billy slipped out the back door and took the long way around, through the woods, down to the water. He sat on his and Benjamin Too's rock and stared out at the lake. Then suddenly he jumped down and began to run to the trees and when he reached a huge old pine tree, he began pounding it with his fists. He didn't stop for a long time. Not until the blood was running from his knuckles. He stopped, then, and a lump the size of a golf ball grew in his throat. His eyes smarted and tears began to seep out.

He was rubbing his eyes and getting pretty mad again when all at once he knew Benjamin Too was there. His voice was sharp, "Where were you? You were supposed to be here."

"What's the matter?"

Usually Billy told his twin everything. Nearly. He said, "Mom and Dad. They think I'm weird."

Benjamin Too wasn't a kidder. But for once, he reached out of his cloud and tapped Billy on the shoulder and said, "Naw. They don't think you're weird. They think you're strange."

Billy snapped. "Stop it! It's not funny! They were talking about me when they didn't know I was there. They never talk about anything anymore and then when they do, it's about me. Like I was something from another planet."

"Aw, Billy, they didn't mean anything. They love you. You can't just quit loving a person. They used to love us, and they said so all the time. Remember? Well, just because I'm gone, that doesn't mean they can just stop loving somebody."

"You've got that right, Benjamin Too." Billy's voice was squeaky. "They love *Baby!* That's who they love. And that's all they love. They don't care if I live or die. They'd like it if I died, too, and then they'd be happy, just the three of them, Mom, Dad and Baby." He was on his feet, and he whirled and put his face close to Benjamin Too's cloud. "I hate them. I hate them. And I hate Baby the most. If they hadn't decided they wanted to—to replace you," there, he'd said it, "then everything would be okay."

Benjamin Too looked at the ground. "I would still be dead."

"But *I'd* still have you...the way you are now. That's okay. I like that okay. And then I'd have you all to myself without them sticking their noses into things. You and me. We'd be having fun. But we can't have fun when they're up there talking about me." He turned and looked out over the water and was quieter when he said, "Saying rotten bad stinky things about me."

Benjamin Too went to stand beside the rock, close to Billy. Billy felt the warmth of the cloud. It helped. But then a thought came to him. Why hadn't he thought of it before? It wasn't fair! Not fair that Benjamin Too—the old Benjamin Too—had died and been replaced by Baby! That was a stinking thing for them to do. Like you could just replace a person with another person, like the first person was just garbage, like an old milk carton or something. Why should the old Benjamin Too be gone and Baby be here, all pink and soft and happy? And taking all of his mom and dad's love.

"I know what to do, Benjamin Too." Billy's voice was sure and solid. And it scared Benjamin Too. "It's the only answer. When it's done, there will be just you and me, and mom and dad, again. It will be just like it was before." His face shone with happiness. Why didn't I think of it before?"

"What?"

"You'll see. You'll see."

All at once Benjamin Too felt sick at his stomach. And scared. He was pretty sure that whatever it was that he came back for was getting closer. He didn't want it to get to him. As quickly as he could, he faded away.

There was a little boat. A simple row boat. Billy sometimes rowed it out across the water. His folks didn't care. He was a good swimmer, they said. Other boys who were eight like Billy weren't allowed to go out in boat by themselves, even if they were good swimmers. But Billy knew the difference: his folks wouldn't care if he drowned. They didn't give a hoot what happened to him. He bet if he was drowning, they wouldn't come and save him. They'd save Baby. But they wouldn't save him. It made him want to hurt them. And now he knew what to do. He knew what to do to hurt them most.

It had been a long day for Billy. He could hardly wait for night when his folks would be asleep and Baby would be asleep in her crib. But mainly it had been long because Benjamin Too hadn't shown up. Not at all.

Yesterday down at the water when he'd first had his idea, he had almost told his brother what his plan was. But then he realized that Benjamin Too would hate it. And that maybe he wouldn't come back and help him. Or come back at all. And so he'd kept quiet. But Benjamin Too knew anyway. Benjamin Too knew things sometimes, things that he wouldn't have known before he died.

Just the same, Billy was excited. Even if Benjamin Too knew, what did it matter? Once Billy had done what he was going to do, things would be okay again. He was sure that Benjamin Too would come back. Sometime. It might be a while, but sometime, Benjamin Too would come back, because his brother loved him. Billy knew that much. And once

Billy had done the thing, then he'd get his folks back, too. They'd notice him again. And then he'd have Benjamin Too and his parents. It would be perfect.

They'd already had supper and his mom and dad, as usual, were in the big room of the cabin, so wrapped up in watching Baby toddle about that they didn't even know Billy was alive. He sat in the folding chair on the porch for a while, then wandered down to the water to look at the boat just one more time. He'd brought it back to the little dock and tied it up. The oars were in it. The water was pretty low, and that meant that he'd have to jump down into it with her, and he'd have to be careful not to drop her.

He was thinking about that when he realized it was dumb. He laughed under his breath so his parents wouldn't hear. What did it matter? If it happened there, or way out on the lake? The end would be the same.

He waited a while, then he got up and went through the big room—neither of his parents looked up because they were watching Baby play with checkers on the coffee table—to the kitchen and noisily opened the cabinet door and got a glass. Then he turned the water on, big, and while it ran, he took the flashlight out of the corner cupboard and pushed it into his pocket and pulled his sweat shirt down over it. He figured that if his parents cared about him, they would notice it as he went back through the big room to the porch. But they didn't care about him and they wouldn't bother to look at him.

He was right.

He sat on the porch again. It seemed forever before he heard his mom tell Baby to kiss Daddy goodnight. It was quiet in the cabin for a time, then his mom came back into the big room and he heard her say, "She went right down. She's so sweet, isn't she? All you have to do is give her her blanket and put her binkie in her mouth, and she's a perfect baby." Billy took note. He'd have to remember that later.

He squirmed in the chair and rubbed his face with his hands. He couldn't help looking around once in a while for Benjamin Too. It wasn't going to stop him from doing what he was going to do if Benjamin Too didn't show up, but he really wished he would. It was really important what he was going to do, and that made it important that his brother be with him.

The moon came up over the lake and after a while there were stars. Finally he heard his mom's voice. "Come in, now, Billy. Time to go to bed." When they were in the city, during school, he had to go to bed early, but when they were at the cabin, he could stay up later. And his mom and dad went to bed earlier when they were at the cabin. He knew that by the time he got a shower and got into bed, they'd be in bed, too. And asleep. But he wouldn't be alseep. He smiled.

He kept sitting up and looking around the room, but pretty soon he quit hoping Benjamin Too would show up. He was going to do what he was going to do, no matter what, so he quit worrying about it. He just waited.

He checked the "glow face" of his watch for the umpteenth time. Five minutes to midnight. Close enough. He got out of his pajamas and into the sweatshirt and jeans he'd worn earlier in the day. The flashlight was still in the pocket. He put on sneakers and socks. He crept to his open door and listened. Nothing.

Slowly, slowly, slowly, without making the slightest sound, he sneaked down the hall to Baby's room. His folks always left her door open so they could hear if she cried, and their door open, too. He would have to work silently. He hesitated at the threshold and switched the flashlight on to check for sure there wasn't anything on the floor he'd trip over and make a noise. Nope. Nothing. He turned the light off and tiptoed to the crib. There he experienced the first problem that he hadn't previously thought out. It would make a noise if he put the crib side down, and he didn't think he could get Baby out unless he did. She was heavy, and she'd wake and probably cry. Nothing for it, though, but to try. He never knew he could be so careful, and once there was a sound. But it wasn't very loud. He stopped and listened. He heard the rustling of bed clothes as one of his parents turned over in bed. Then it was quiet again. Baby slept on.

It seemed an eternity before the crib side was down, and he had very, very carefully let go of it.

Now. Get the binkie into Baby's mouth so she wouldn't cry out. And get that filthy old blanket she couldn't live without so when he picked her up, she wouldn't cry. He couldn't take the chance of saying anything to her, even in a whisper. One short beam of the flashlight and he saw the binkie where it had fallen out of Baby's mouth, and the blanket was bunched up around her feet. He hoped it wasn't tangled.

He did it all in one move. Into the mouth went the binkie as he gathered the blanket and lifted the baby and in absolute silence, taking long, soft steps, made it to the end of the hall. His hand pressed the binkie into Baby's mouth. She was struggling, but she wasn't making any noise. Into the kitchen where there was a nightlight, and out the back door onto the screened porch. Still he didn't dare take his hand off the baby's face.

The screen door would squeak unless he was careful. He knew that. And so it took him minutes, long minutes, to coax it open and get them through it. Then down the back steps and into the woods.

Once they were a good ways into the forest, he took his hand off Baby's face and she began to fuss. Not loud yet, so he comforted her with words and strokes to her face. He stuck the binkie back in her mouth. "It's okay, Baby. It's okay. Billy's taking you for a walk." She whimpered for a moment but when Billy turned the flashlight on she was fascinated with the skittering pool of light. He was breathing hard. Baby was heavier than he thought.

He sucked in a long, deep breath, shifted the baby's weight, and began walking down the slope toward the lake. He hadn't gone very far when he knew that Benjamin Too was beside him. His heart filled with sunshine. He wanted to hug him, but his arms were full. "Benjamin Too," he whispered, "you came."

"Yeah." Billy expected more from his brother, but Benjamin Too wasn't talking much. They walked silently toward the dock where the mud was thick and slimy. Soon their shoes were covered with muck. Billy sat on the edge of the dock and said, "Here, help me with Baby. She's real heavy."

Benjamin Too just stood there for so long that Billy looked up at him. "What're you waiting for? Take her for a minute." Benjamin Too didn't hurry, but he did sit down beside Billy and they transferred the baby to his arms. It was quiet and dark. The only sound was the 'suck, suck' of Baby and the pacifier.

When Billy's breath was even again, he said, "The boat's tied to the end of the dock."

"What're you doing, Billy?" Benjamin Too said, but Billy knew as sure as he'd ever known anything before, that Benjamin Too knew.

"You know."

"What?"

"You know. I have to, Benjamin Too."

"No, Billy, you don't have to."

"Yes I do. It's not my fault that nobody loves me. It's not my fault that mom and dad would just as soon I'd be on the moon. They wish it was me that died. And then when they couldn't fix that, they had Baby so they could pretend I don't even exist. So, you see, Benjamin Too, I got to do it."

Benjamin Too's eyes had filled with tears. He knew that there was some truth in what Billy said, and he loved his twin. Twins were very, very close, even if one of them was dead. But that didn't mean you had to help your twin do something as bad as what Billy was planning to do.

"We'll figure out something else, Billy."

That made Billy mad. "*What* else? What d'ya think I've been trying to figure for the last two years? There isn't anything else. This is it, and if you don't want to help me, then just go away." He was suddenly panicked that Benjamin Too would and he watched carefully. But although Benjamin Too's cloud vibrated and turned a nasty color, he didn't go anywhere. It was a few minutes before Billy was sure.

"Okay, Benjamin Too," he said, "the water's low so you gotta help me. I'll get down in the boat and then you can hand Baby down to me. Okay?"

Benjamin Too's cloud looked muddy and got swirls of ugly stuff in it. Then it began to wiggle and that made Billy nervous, but he figured that if he hurried and didn't give Benjamin Too a chance to think too much, it would be okay. He ran to the end of the dock and turned to wait. Benjamin was taking his good old time getting there, but Billy didn't say anything. Benjamin Too came up close with the baby who began to wave her arms and kick. Benjamin Too struggled with her, and somehow the binkie fell out of Baby's mouth. She began to cry.

"Dammit. Dammit all to hell, find the binkie," Billy said. He jumped off the edge of the dock and hit the bottom of the boat with a thud. Quickly he reached up for the baby. Benjamin Too was holding the heavy, squirming child, and looking for the binkie. Finally he found it. But his face didn't look happy.

"Give her to me," Billy said. Benjamin Too went to his knees on the dock and leaned down to give the baby to Billy. She was fussing louder. Billy was standing straddle-legged, trying to balance himself, but he was reaching up high and the boat began to rock under him. He got hold of the baby, then sat down hard and fast. He bumped one of the oars and it slapped into the water, splashing them. The baby gasped and began waving her little arms as the cold water hit her face and the binkie went into the lake. She began to cry in earnest. Billy was frantic. They were quite a long way from the cabin, but over the water, and in the night, noises carried.

"Get in the boat, Benjamin Too," he hissed, and in a panic, stuck his finger in the baby's mouth. She began to suck on it, making a lot of noise, but at least she stopped crying.

Benjamin Too was still on the dock.

"Get in the boat, Benjamin Too."

But Benjamin Too didn't. He stood there.

It was dark on the water, but Billy saw that Benjamin Too's cloud had some kind of blackish stuff working around in it, and Billy could see that Benjamin Too wasn't happy. His cloud was so dark that Billy couldn't really see what his brother's face looked like. For the first time in the long evening, Billy was getting scared. Not about what he was going to do with Baby, but that he might lose Benjamin Too because of it.

"Come on, Benjamin Too. I need you." He'd used that before and it always worked with his twin. Benjamin Too had some kind of a right-and-wrong button, and Billy knew just what pushed it. He said it again, more softly, "I need you, Benjamin Too. I love you."

Benjamin Too sat down on the edge of the dock and then dropped into the boat. Billy reached out to pat him on the back with the hand that wasn't in the baby's mouth, but Benjamin Too in his cloud seemed to shy away.

"Row the boat out to the middle, Benjamin Too."

The black icky stuff in Benjamin Too's cloud swirled around. But he managed to get the oars and began to row.

"Keep goin'," Billy said, peering past Benjamin Too and the cloud. They were in the middle of the quiet lake when he said, "Okay. This'll be all right."

Benjamin Too fastened the oars into the locks. He still didn't speak. Billy pulled his finger out of Baby's mouth and she looked around, her eyes bright.

Billy suddenly had the thought that perhaps Benjamin Too would betray him. Aw, he wouldn't do that. But he might. Billy stared at his twin, his eyes narrowed. Would he? Billy decided he wouldn't, that Benjamin Too knew what Billy needed, that Billy needed to be the only thing in his parent's lives. And Benjamin Too, in the end, always did his best to see that Billy got what he needed. And Billy knew the right words to say if it looked like his brother might try to stop what he was going to do. He'd say, "Benajmin Too, I love you. I need you, Benjamin Too." Billy smiled then. But, just in case, Billy decided to swim out a ways from the boat before he let the baby go, far enough that Benjamin Too couldn't reach her in case he had some kind of an urge to pull her out of the water.

Billy said, "Hold her a minute, Benjamin Too." He handed the baby to him, took off his sneakers and slid quietly over the side into the water. Benjamin Too was staring down at the baby in his arms. She smiled and said, "Goo." Benjamin Too smiled back at her. His cloud got gold speckles in it, and whooshed around a little.

Billy said, "Give her to me."

Benjamin Too frowned through the speckles in his cloud that had suddenly turned purple and black. "No."

"Yes. You know why, Benjamin Too. You know it's the only way for me."

"We can do something else."

"No, we can't." Billy gripped the side of the boat, his hands hard and white, and his voice became harsh. "You know it's the only way."

Slowly at first, Benjamin Too's cloud began to pulsate. It was gray now. Muddy gray. He began to move toward Billy but it was awkward because of the baby. Billy watched. Then Benjamin Too freed one hand and quickly snatched an oar from the locks. He let the baby go, and she plopped into the bottom of the boat. With both hands sticking out of his cloud, Benjamin Too brought the edge of the oar down, hard, on first Billy's left hand and then his right. Billy yelled, and let go, and as he did, Benjamin Too's hands, poking out of his cloud, stuck the oar into Billy's chest and pushed off. Billy went under, then came up sputtering and tossing his hair out of his face.

"Benjamin Too! What's the matter with you? You creep, come back." Benjamin Too was busy rearranging the crying baby so she was sitting solidly in the bottom of the boat. Billy was so mad he was crazy, but he wasn't scared. He was a good swimmer, and he began to swim for the boat. He was ready to kill Benjamin Too. He would! Who would know? And Benjamin Too needed killing for this stupid trick.

As he swam toward the boat, he saw that Benjamin Too's cloud was changing again, turning to the stuff like Jell-O. It was green and wiggly. He watched, fascinated but not scared, as Benjamin Too began to pull his cloud off like he was taking off a tee-shirt. Pulled it right over his head, inside out, looked out at Billy, gave a sort of a flip like he was a cowboy twirling a rope or like the guy at the pizza place whirling dough over his head. And then he threw his cloud.

The ugly green thing came down right over Billy's head and he noticed that by that time it was clingy and sticky like a whole bunch of Gummy Bears stuck together. Billy flailed, trying to get it off of him, but it just got heavier and stickier and gummier. It filled up his ears and then it filled up his nose, and he opened his mouth to yell to Benjamin Too, "I need you, Benjamin too. I love you, Benjamin Too" but....

# Wedding at the Gormay Cafe

MAY

May slid into the back booth, stretched her short, plump legs out under the marble-patterned tabletop, and rested her feet on the seat across from her. As she lay her head against the padded back, she sighed. Her hands, a pencil in one, a pad in the other, dropped to the seat beside her. The cooler in the kitchen whirred and the blue neon sign in the window snapped and hissed.

It was the best time of May's day. The noon rush over. The kitchen wiped clean. Mary Frances gone home until five. It would be another half hour before the girls from the telephone office came in for their coffee break. It was just about the only quiet time May had, from five in the morning when she came into The Gormay Cafe, until she went home at eight in the evening, leaving Gordie to take the money from the last customers and see that the girls cleaned up.

Ordinarily May used this time to plan the specials for the next day, but today she had a wedding to think about. After all this time, Mary Frances was getting married. After all these years, Mary Frances Birdsong was going to be a bride. Monday at eleven o'clock, right here in The Gormay Cafe. May straightened up, wet the tip of her pencil in her mouth and wrote: *Pick up chairs at fire hall.* She placed the pencil on the next line, but it wouldn't move. After a moment, her shoulders drooped and her gaze wandered out the big, low, front windows where a couple of little kids bobbed by on their way home from first grade that let out at two-thirty. The minute hand on the Coca Cola clock lurched ahead to the next black mark and May sighed and gave up on the list. She put the pencil down and went to the counter that ran half the length of the cafe and took a coffee cup from the row that sat, clean and shining, on a folded towel. She filled it and, holding it between her hands, placed her elbows on the counter. Her eyes were on the storefront across the empty afternoon street, but she didn't even know she was looking at it.

Something was wrong. May wasn't happy about Mary Frances getting married, and that made her ashamed. But it was the truth, and although she had been careful not to let Mary Frances know how she felt, there wasn't any use denying it. It was taking all the joy out of what should be one of the happiest times of her life. She loved Mary Frances. They were more than just friends. Mary Frances was like another part of May, that's how close they were. They had shared their lives. Everything. Except for that one thing that happened on graduation night—my goodness, could it be twenty-two years ago?—that something so awful that Mary Frances never to this day had talked about it. Except for that, they had shared everything. They had seen each other almost every day of their lives since they were five years old.

And so May knew when something was wrong.

She sipped her black coffee, tightened her lips and shook her head. Shoot. Maybe she was just getting all bothered about something that didn't amount to anything. The important thing was that Mary Frances was getting married. Wasn't that what counted? Wasn't that what they'd always dreamed about, the two of them, ever since they played dolls in the empty garage that sat on the shady alley between their back yards? Hadn't they talked, like little girls do, about growing up and getting married and having two babies each and living next door to each other in new houses?

They had. They had pretended and dreamed. But, until now, only half the dream had come true. May's half. She married Gordie Johannsen less than a year out of high school and the next year she had Jimmy. And when he was two, right on schedule, Bobby came along. It took longer to get the new house, but last year, when Bobby got out of school, Gordie had finally built her a nice three-bedroom ranch-style out on Grange Road. He'd always said he wasn't going to build a new house as long as those boys were home to tear it up.

May had everything, a good husband, two fine boys, a new house and a money-making little business, while Mary Frances didn't have a blessed thing. Well, that wasn't altogether so. Mary Frances had her job here at The Gormay, and that big old house, plus her savings. She always said there wasn't anything she wanted to spend her money on, anyway, except on things for May and Gordie's boys. She had been more than generous with them, even offering to help with their tuition to state college.

For their part, May and Gordie had gone out of their way to make Mary Frances a part of their family, especially after her mother died. They had included her in all the birthdays and Christmases and summer picnics, and one summer they all took a vacation together and went to The Grand Canyon. She'd been such a part of their family that she'd taken her turn sitting with the boys when they were sick, just like May and Gordie did. May knew that Mary Frances loved those boys like they were her own. But, she knew, too, that it wasn't enough. It wasn't what a person like Mary Frances deserved. She deserved the best.

What she was getting wasn't even close to the best. Clarence Peavy wasn't good enough for Mary Frances. Nowhere near good enough. Suddenly, May looked at the ceiling and snorted delicately. So what if *she* didn't like Clarence?

Wasn't any of her business who Mary Frances decided to marry. May's eyes filled with tears and she reached in her pocket and got a Kleenex and blew her nose. It was, too. It was her business because she loved Mary Frances and couldn't stand for her to settle for second best. And Clarence Peavy wasn't even that. When it came to "best," Clarence was at the bottom of the list.

May wasn't really able to put her finger on what was wrong with Clarence. Lots of little things, but nothing big. He was as good as most men around town. He was clean. He paid his bills. Kept up his place. And he didn't smoke or drink as far as May knew. He had waited six months after his wife died before he called on Mary Frances or even made out like he wanted to. And you had to give him credit for that, because, living next door to her the way he did, he could have been a real pest.

Lost in her thoughts, May sipped her coffee. Maybe she didn't like Clarence because he had an eye for the ladies. Just an eye, mind you. Nobody had ever said anything about him fooling around. But May had seen him ogling Betty Lou Hooper right here in The Gormay Cafe when he didn't know she was watching, and it made her uneasy. Of course, Betty Lou was asking for it. Up until recently May had felt sorry for Betty Lou. In high school they'd voted her the Most Popular Girl. She had naturally curly red hair and a good figure and a good personality. Then she'd gone off and married some good-for-nothing who drank up everything he made and finally left her. She had come back to Cedar City then, looking twenty years older than she was. But when she finally got her divorce, she'd touched up the gray hairs and bought false eye lashes, then hemmed up her skirts and inch and a half, and started flouncing around town like the Queen of Sheba. Betty Lou was looking for a man. She didn't say so, of course, but any single woman who wore scoop-necks so low you could see half way to her navel when she bent over, was certainly not planning on spending the rest of her life sleeping by herself. May supposed any man would look (she kept a sharp eye on Gordie when Betty Lou was around) and Clarence probably wasn't any worse than the rest of them.

The fact was, there were just two unmarried women in town, other than teenagers, that any man would look at twice. Mary Frances and Betty Lou. And as much as it pained her, May admitted that Betty Lou with her oversized boobs pooched out of her scoop neck, her bleached hair and high heels, had a lot more of what most men were looking for than Mary Frances. Mary Frances was pretty in her own way, but there was just something about a woman like Betty Lou who's got *come-and-get-it-or-I'm-throwin'-it-out* in her eyes that makes fools out of men.

So when Clarence came courting Mary Frances instead of Betty Lou, May couldn't help wondering if it was because Betty Lou didn't have a pot or a window, either, while Mary Frances had a nice big house and a good job. He probably even knew about her savings. There weren't many secrets in Cedar City. It was just a short while after Mary Frances and Clarence announced their engagement that Betty Lou came into a little bit of money from a rich uncle or somebody, and at first, May had wished that Clarence would just throw Mary Frances over for Betty Lou. But when she thought about how that would make Mary Frances look, and how it would hurt her, she changed her mind.

Without knowing she was doing it, May reached behind her for the damp dishcloth and wiped a spot away from the countertop. She put the cloth back, took a swallow of her coffee and reset her elbows on the counter. She should be more careful about her opinions of people. She didn't know for a fact that Clarence had ever had any designs on Mary Frances's house and savings, and that little picture she had in her mind of Clarence lounging around all day while Mary Frances came to work was just something she'd thought up when she was feeling spiteful.

Clarence was new to town, and maybe that's what May didn't like about him. It wasn't really a prejudice, she told herself, but she held some hard feelings against outsiders. Hardly anyone moved into or out of Cedar City and the farmers outside town never moved at all. Generation after generation stayed on, working longer and harder every year, what with prices for everything except their crops going up. Most of the jobs in town depended directly or indirectly on the farmers, so if someone new came in, it meant that somebody already living in town would lose out some way.

Clarence had shown up in Cedar City about two years ago, a few months after Mr. Walker died, asking how to get to Mrs. Walker's place. Agnes Walker lived next door to Mary Frances in a house almost exactly like hers. Clarence had knocked on Agnes's door and said he was a friend of her brother in St. Louis.

The upshot was that Clarence and Agnes were married eight months after her husband died, in spite of the fact that Agnes was a number of years older and had a bad heart, and Clarence knew it. Agnes never *had* had much sense and she was silly over Clarence. She told everybody that Clarence said he wanted them to have as much time together as the Good Lord would give them. Well, the Lord made it clear that he didn't have much time in mind, because she died only about three months after they were married. Of course, Clarence got the house and whatever else she had, which wasn't much. You couldn't say that Clarence had done anything wrong, and everybody had to admit that he had been good to Agnes while she was alive.

May took a good look at her own thoughts. Except for that one little thing—that Clarence was inclined to look at the ladies a little too much and too long—she didn't have any good excuse to feel the way she did. He was only ten years older than Mary Frances. True, he was shorter, but being short wasn't something you ought to hold against a man. Gordie was only five-eight, but still, he was six inches taller than May. Clarence wasn't a fraction of an inch taller than Mary Frances. His face was jowly and red, and he was always sweating. He laughed too loud, and lots of times May couldn't figure out what was so funny. What hair he had he parted just above his left ear so he could pull a few strands across the top of his head and plaster them down with Creme

Glow Hair Dressing. But he always opened the car door for Mary Frances, and pulled her chair out for her when they had their regular Thursday night dinner at The Gormay on Mary Frances's day off, and he had given her a nice little diamond ring. Everybody knew he had a railroad pension, and now, of course, there was Agnes's house that they could have for a rental, so it wasn't as if he had nothing at all to offer Mary Frances. And, shoot, all men looked at ladies, especially ones got up like Betty Lou.

May muttered aloud, "Clarence Peavy's not that bad." After all, beggars couldn't be choosers, and while Mary Frances certainly hadn't gone out begging, she was past the point of being too choosey.

May felt her throat tighten up and got the Kleenex out of her pocket and pressed it against her nose. She had had such hopes for Mary Frances. She hated so bad, after all these years, to have to give them up. Oh, of course, it wasn't likely that Mary Frances would ever have any children, no matter who she married. But, still, with the right man—someone from around Cedar City that they all had something in common with—someone she and Gordie and the boys could have felt easy with—well, it would have been nice.

May stuffed the Kleenex back in her pocket and smiled to herself. At least Mary Frances would finally get to use the things out of her hope chest, the cedar chest her mother had passed down to her. All those things they'd hemmed and embroidered during the long summers. The linens May had put away were long gone, ragged and stained and washed to pieces over the years, but Mary Frances's tablecloths and doilies and towels were still nice. May remembered those afternoons when they sat in the porch swing with their needlework. Oh, how they'd talked! About everything under the sun, but mostly about boys.

Their hope chests were pretty full by the time they were seniors, and about that time boys began to ask May for dates. Toward the end of the year, she started going steady with Gordie. Even then, when she and Gordie got so thick right around graduation, May and Mary Frances saw each other every day before school and during classes and every afternoon, so they hadn't drifted apart.

May had wished that Mary Frances would get a boy friend, too, so they could double date. But boys just didn't go for Mary Frances mainly because she was so tall. There were only two boys in the whole senior class as tall as Mary Frances, and one of them was Chuck Whaley, student body president and captain of the football team, and Mary Frances didn't have a chance with him. Besides, she had been so skinny that nobody ever noticed what big, soft brown eyes she had and how thick and shiny her dark brown hair was. She just didn't have any sex appeal to attract the boys. Thinking about Mary Frances's flat hips and thin legs, May slid her hand along the generous thigh that bulged beneath her white waitress dress.

Mary Frances had one date. Graduation night. May closed her eyes and lowered her head when she thought about it. It was twenty-two years ago, and whatever happened that night had marked Mary Frances forever. May shook her head. They had been so excited when, just a week before graduation, Dwayne Linfers had come up to them in the hall, his face the color of a beet, and asked Mary Frances to go out with him after the ceremonies. May had been relieved, because she had been about to ask Gordie if they could take Mary Frances with them on their date and she knew he would balk at that. Gordie was getting impatient about things and he wanted them to be alone so his hands could wander. May wouldn't let him go too far, but she kind of liked Gordie's wandering hands.

After school that day she and Mary Frances went up to Mary Frances's bedroom and lay across her bed and talked and giggled. They wondered how Dwayne had ever got up the nerve to speak to a girl, much less ask one for a date. If it was possible, he was more bashful than Mary Frances, and for sure he was skinnier. But, even if he was all knees and elbows, he was four inches taller and had the nicest sparkly blue eyes. He was polite and smart, too. On the Honor Roll, and played French horn in the band.

May and Mary Frances had spent the last week before graduation planning every last detail of what they would wear under the gray graduation gowns, and trying out new lipsticks and hair styles. They had gone to the city together and May got a pale mint green dress with a white collar that pointed up her fair complexion and blond page boy. They'd about given up before they found the dusty rose crepe dress that fit Mary Frances and was long enough, too. It was perfect with her dark hair and eyes.

Then they went home, opened the packages and waited for the boys to call and find out what colors their dresses were so they could send corsages that went with them. Gordie called—May found out later he didn't know he was supposed to until his mom told him—and she and Mary Frances guessed that he would send yellow roses. It turned out they were right. But Dwayne never did even call. They were scared to death he'd bring red carnations that would clash with the dusty rose dress.

On the big night, Dwayne still hadn't called, and May had run over to Mary Frances's house the very last thing before she and Gordie left for the auditorium, because she was dying to know what Dwayne had brought. But he hadn't come yet, so she had to go on without knowing.

At the school, in the home ec room, all the time she was putting her corsage in the refrigerator and getting her gown and cap on right, she kept watching the door for Mary Frances. And then there she was! And on the dusty rose dress was a white orchid. There was only one other orchid corsage that night—the purple one Chuck Whaley gave Betty Lou Hooper—and Mary Frances's orchid was bigger.

May hadn't been able to find her tongue at first. She just stood there looking at Mary Frances. A *different* Mary Frances. She was beautiful. There wasn't any other word for it. All the other girls stared, too, and for a minute, the room was silent.

After the ceremonies, when they were standing on the back steps of the auditorium waiting for their dates, May had felt like Mary Frances was Cinderella. She just kept staring at her, and Mary Frances looked back at her as if she knew, too, that for the very first time, she was beautiful. May had almost cried with happiness for her when Dwayne came up in his new suit and took her arm and they walked away toward the parking lot. They looked like James Stewart and Olivia de Haviland.

Behind May the clock ticked and she felt the corn on her toe hurting. She turned and warmed up her coffee in the microwave and took it back to the booth. For the millionth time, she wondered what happened that night between Mary Frances and Dwayne. Time after time she had started to ask, but then she would remember the hurt in Mary Frances's eyes that next morning, and she had never had the heart to bring it up.

The morning after graduation May hadn't even eaten breakfast before she ran across the alley and into the Birdsong kitchen. Mrs. Birdsong told her Mary Frances hadn't come downstairs yet, so May ran up and burst into her room like she had all her life. But as soon as she opened the door, she could feel it. Something awful had happened. There was something in Mary Frances's eyes that had never been there before, and it made May feel sick inside even before they spoke. Just thinking about it made May's eyes fill up and she fumbled for the damp Kleenex again. Whatever it was that had made Mary Frances beautiful the night before was gone, and she had never looked like that again.

May had asked her what was wrong, but Mary Frances just shook her head and turned away, fiddling with her hair brush, and said, "Nothing." The white orchid was on the dresser and May asked Mary Frances if she wasn't going to put it in the refrigerator, and Mary Frances looked at her for a second like she didn't remember who she was, then kind of nodded her head and said, oh yes, she guessed she would. May remembered that they'd stood there a long time with a big silence between them. May had kept opening her mouth to ask what was wrong, but she'd stop, just before the words came out. She was Mary Frances's best friend, and best friends don't try to pump a person who doesn't want to talk. They just try to be there. Just stay close.

So May had stayed close to Mary Frances and had done her best to keep her busy, which was hard, since there wasn't any school or anything. It was the longest time—weeks and weeks—before May ever heard Mary Frances laugh again. But then she and Gordie set the date, and Mary Frances was going to be Maid of Honor, and she threw herself into the wedding plans as if nothing had ever happened. But May could see it, sometimes, that hurting in the soft brown eyes, and it broke her heart.

They heard later that Dwayne Linfers had enlisted in the Navy the day after graduation, and although it got around a few years ago that he had come back to the Linfers family farm, he never came into Cedar City. The Linfers farm was a long way out, and by the time Dwayne came back, the Interstate had been finished and it was just as easy for him to go into the city as it was to come to Cedar City. Even so, you'd think that he'd have come in for *something*, unless he had some good reason to stay away. May had finally decided that whatever happened that night had something to do with it. They must have had a fight that night, Dwayne and Mary Frances, and he was either mad about it, or he felt guilty, and either way, May didn't much care if he ever showed his face. But, then, she would remember Mary Frances's eyes the morning after graduation and she knew it wasn't like that. It wasn't just a fight. It was something...something terrible.

Mary Frances never mentioned Dwayne Linfers name again. She never had another date. Once in a while, one of the regulars at the Gormay would ask her, but she always turned them down. That is, until Clarence came courting her last year just after her fortieth birthday party. There had been a few times, over the years, when May thought that Mary Frances still liked Dwayne. But that didn't make any sense. Shoot. That was twenty-two years ago. Nobody would wait that long for a man.

But that strange thought had run through May's head

again two weeks ago when she and Mary Frances were making out the wedding invitations. Everybody in their graduating class was invited, of course. There would be plenty of room in the cafe, since there were only about twenty in their class, and Mary Frances didn't have any living relatives. When they came to Dwayne's name that day, May had glanced up at Mary Frances and for a second she thought the big brown eyes were misty. May just looked right back down at the list, and trying to be casual, made a mark through the name.

But Mary France said, "No. It's all right, May. He wouldn't show up anyway." And on her face was the strangest look. May couldn't figure out what it meant.

Well, May had had to agree that Dwayne wouldn't show up, so she put his name on an envelope and put it in the mail with the rest. She got a little catty satisfaction out of sending him the invitation to Mary Frances's wedding, just in case he had some idea she had been waiting around for him for twenty-two years.

May pulled in her breath and brought herself back to the present. Outside there was the sound of a truck shifting down, its engine backfiring, as it came into town. May waited, and watched it go by, and felt the vibration come up through the floor. She glanced at her watch and looked down at the note pad with its one line and thought about the look on Mary Frances's face when they talked about inviting Dwayne. It wasn't angry. Or hateful. May frowned. It was tragic. That's what it was. May just couldn't imagine...after all these years.

The front door opened and the chattering of the telephone girls jarred May out of her thoughts. She put a smile on and went up to the counter. "What'll it be today, girls?" she asked.

## MARY FRANCES

From the honeysuckle that vined along the porches of the big shaded houses came the sweet still smell of summer. As Mary Frances passed, the grass came alive with the buzz and fluttering of insects. Her feet knew all the humps and breaks in the sidewalk where the roots of the great maples had lifted and broken them, and her skin knew the feel of the stupefied air.

It was Mary Frances's habit to walk the four and a half blocks from The Gormay Cafe to her house at this time each day with her mind in a suspended state. It was a time when, without her participation, a minor battle waged far down inside her. The skirmish was necessary because she had to be relocated from the bustling noise and voices of the cafe to the silence of the old house in such a way that she could accept the empty afternoon hours as good. *A private time to savor,* the brave knight of her subconscious would argue; *a time alone because no one wants you,* the evil black dragon would counter. Usually her knight was victorious. Today he had fought weakly and the battle's end was indecisive.

So her step was slow as she approached the gate in the low wire fence around her own yard. Snowball, asleep in the porch swing, stood, blinked, and arched her back in elaborate disinterest. Mary Frances opened the heavy door and went inside. She paused to let the cat enter, then, out of respect for the town's quiet time, closed the door softly behind her. Faint blue daylight seeped through the small cherub-etched oval glass of the door and it was cool and dim in the hall.

She sat on the oak bench and Snowball leapt up beside her. The silence ran on as she stroked the silken fur. Then she bent, untied her thick-soled white oxfords, removed them and placed them beside her on the seat. There they would be when it was time for her to return to the cafe for her five-to-eight shift.

In her stockinged feet she padded down the hall, into the kitchen, and put the kettle on for tea. She bent to check the level of the blue flame then went through the open door to the screened back porch. It smelled of the cluster rose that climbed the cornerpost, and of the dust that gathered on it, and of the rich soil in a flat of fall-bearing tomato plants on the floor. She rearranged the cushion in the old wicker chair and lowered herself into its comfort. Furtively, so that she herself would not notice, she glanced next door and saw that Clarence's car was gone, and did not acknowledge the relief that puffed through her, disintegrated and scattered like dandelion spores.

She closed her eyes. Her long graceful hands, their skin reddened by the strong soap that kept The Gormay Cafe sanitary, opened and closed. Five days. Five days until her wedding. Suddenly her hands rose and covered her face, then, just as abruptly, went back to grip the arms of the chair, and she lifted her head high. No, Mary Frances. Too late, Mary Frances. There's no turning back now. It's decided. And when it is done, you will have peace. Sweet peace.

The thought quieted her. Honeybees droned in the cluster rose. From somewhere, perhaps an old garage on an alley, came the sound of children at play. Sparrows in the elm tree chirped and in the distance a dog barked. To the summer chorus the teakettle added its shrill obbligato. Mary Frances went to the kitchen and took a flowered cup and saucer from the shelf, poured hot water over a tea bag and returned to her place in the wicker chair.

"In five days, they can no longer call me a spinster," she said aloud. She moved the words about in her mouth, playing them off her teeth with her tongue, and her grip on the saucer eased. In five days she would be a married woman, like the other women of Cedar City. Like the normal women of Cedar City.

Oh, but it had been close. She had come very close to living out her life in her own strange and solitary way. In the lovely, secret little prison to which she had committed herself so long ago. For years and years after that night *(Oh, God, that night)* she had existed on her hope. All those long first years she had thought there would be a letter. Then the time came when she knew she was wrong, and like a sensible woman, she tried to put her hope away. She would put it out and close the door, but the moment it cried, she would throw open the door and take it in the circle of her arms, and at night, she would stroke it and nuzzle it and take its small comforts because she was too weak to let it go. It was then that the gray ocean began to churn so close that the waves licked at her feet.

So, in desperation, she had fashioned her fantasyland and she went there when hope threatened her. There she had love and beauty. It was a secret place, hers alone, and she guarded it carefully because it was as fragile as sugar garlands on a wedding cake, and would shatter if the pearlescent walls of the secret hiding place were breached.

She had found a kind of contentment for a time, even rushing back to her solitude sometimes, but, then, seven years ago—or is it eight, now?—came the shred of news. They were saying he had come back to his family's farm. Like a lion from a broken cage, her hope charged again. And again it died. The hungry tide that had receded from her fairyland isle came roaring in and swirled around her feet. She sloshed through it for months and became as thin as a cadaver, and May made her stay home in bed for a week. But that had been a mistake. There alone, without the hand and mind-occupying bustle of The Gormay Cafe, she had become friendly with the ocean, and flirted with its tempting offer of everlasting peace in trade for one moment of pain. It was a long, long time before she was able to climb up on the sparkling beach of her fantasy again.

Then, one day everything changed. It was the day before her fortieth birthday and she had been sitting in this very chair, drinking her tea, thinking about the party May had planned for her, when she felt herself stand up, out of her own body, and go over and sit on the old kitchen chair with the broken slat, and look back at herself. She saw a woman whose life was half gone, and who had sacrificed half of that to a fantasy. A fantasy that had no more chance of coming to fruit than poor spayed Snowball had of producing kittens.

That day she had been surprised to realize that there might be another life—a real one—that she could choose. She had seen herself standing at the top of a ridge and had known that it was time to start down the other side. There were lots of roads leading off the ridge, but it was easy to see the one she should take. All the others led off into forests, or mists, or fading twilights, *(and one, oh, God, one into a fairyland)* but the right one was straight and well-marked and well-lit. There were no trees or flowers along its shoulder, and it had no special points of interest, and there was no scenic wonder at its end, but that day when she was brimming over with good sense, she had known those things didn't matter, anyway.

What mattered were her responsibilities. She had a responsibility to God who had entrusted a life to her which she had let lie fallow for twenty-two years. She had a responsibility to herself, too. She needed a real *living* life. But what she had seen most clearly of all was that she had a responsbility to May, never mind God and herself. In truth, the responsibility to May had gone far beyond that in twenty-two years, and now it was a debt.

For without May, Mary Frances never would have made it to the top of that ridge. May had been at her side every day since that awful time *(that night, that night of joy and terror and shame)* urging her along, tugging gently once in a while when Mary Frances wandered too close to the crashing ocean of the bewildering secret that licked at the edges of her sanity. She'd kept her eye on Mary Frances, and during the worst times, the first few months after graduation *(that night)* and again seven years ago—eight, now—when the ocean's waves came crashing up after her, May had been right there, hanging on. She never let go. May had saved Mary Frances. Saved her from her own silly self.

Mary Frances had been ashamed when she saw that all those years she had accepted May's goodness and love as something she had coming, like her paycheck. She had let her friend take her into her own family like an adopted child, and Mary Frances knew, on that day before she turned forty, that it was all wrong. She was as awkward as an extra arm or leg. Like a deformity. She had deformed May's perfect family. Made what was natural unnatural. May—and Gordie and the boys—they all deserved better.

Mary Frances sipped her tea and shook her head. There must have been a time when May wondered if she were worth all the trouble. Then Mary Frances's eyes stung with tears. May would never think something like that. But Mary Frances had. Many times she had wondered if it was worth the energy it took to keep her life going when all it had to feed on was pointlessness. On that day before she turned forty, she thanked God that she hadn't given up. She could still make it right with Him, and herself, and most important of all, with her friend. And she would.

She started by forcing herself to put into words that she could say aloud to herself, a explanation of what had happened that night. They were these:

That night, the two of them, Mary Frances Birdsong and Dwayne Linfers, were supposed to have been bound together for all their lives. But something had gone wrong. God had blinked, or Fate had been distracted for an instant, or there was some malfunction of the universe, and in the confusion, things got out of control for a few minutes. When it was over, the two of them still existed as one, all right, but in two joined parts. Between the right and left parts of the one being there was a thick, solid, but transparent wall of shame and guilt. Mary Frances could see Dwayne through it, and she supposed he could see her, too, but they couldn't hear each other's cries, and they couldn't break through the wall. It wasn't their fault. It wasn't anybody's fault. Something just went wrong, and they were caught in it, and, as a result, they were separated but not released from each other. For all those long years she thought the separation was only of their bodies, and not meant to be of their souls, too. But on that day she saw she had been foolish about that. Anyone who was honest with herself could see that the accident was too terrible to survive.

So, on that day before she was forty, she had put her fantasy away. It was like folding away a loved and beautiful dress that had faded and become frayed and gone out of style. She had wrapped it in the delicate tissue of memories and laid it away with care, and for a time she carried the sad weight of its loss.

Snowball stirred beside Mary Frances and she rose and

took her cup and saucer into the kitchen, rinsed them, and placed them in the sink. She turned the white porcelain knob on the range, and watched the flame die under the teakettle, then went through the dark hall and up the stairs.

At the open door of the spare room she paused. The pretty white satin-back crepe dress that May had helped her pick out lay across the bed. Beside it were two open boxes. One held her flat white slippers, and the other, the band adorned with silk rosebuds and lilies-of-the-valley that she would clip on her dark hair come Monday. The flowers were fastened with white ribbon and it was like the ribbon that tied a white orchid once upon a time. Abruptly she put the lid on the box and left the room.

In her own bedroom she went to the window and stood while she arranged her thoughts. She smiled a little. On Monday, everything would be different for her. After that day the men who sat at the counter at The Gormay Cafe couldn't tease her. "Any woman who can make a cup of coffee like this would've made some man a good wife," they'd say, as if it were too late. "How come you want to be an old maid, Mary Frances? You're too pretty for that," one of them would say, and turn and wink at the others, and she would feel heat rise to her face because she knew it wasn't so. "Yep. Too bad ol' Mary Frances never found herself a good man."

Next week it would all be different, she thought as she went down the hall and into her own bedroom. She ran her hand down the lace curtain at the window. Why, even this old house would have a new life. She would have friends and neighbors in. She would invite May and Gordie and the boys for Thanksgiving dinner at the big dining table. There would be a Christmas tree and summer potlucks in the back yard under the shade trees. And maybe she could have a wedding shower for Jimmy's girl one of these days. That would be nice.

Yes, thought Mary Frances Birdsong, it's the kind of life she would have that counted. Love wasn't necessary. She had already loved *(and loves, even now, the voice said, and she stilled it angrily)* and didn't need to love again. She had watched the married couples of Cedar City as they dined in The Gormay Cafe, and she knew they weren't in love, yet they seemed to be all right. When the voice inside her started to speak again, she turned away from the window and went to the dresser and busied her hands with the mirror and the hair brush, so that she wasn't sure she heard it at all. *"You could never love again. It would be disloyal. Disloyal, Mary Frances,"* it might have said. *"Don't cry, Mary Frances."*

A car went by outside and she whirled to go to the window but turned away before she got there and sat on the bed, her hand gripping the bedpost. In a moment she drew her breath in. Being married was the important thing. At eleven o'clock on Monday, she would become Mrs. Clarence Peavy. May would have the cafe decorated with roses and peonies and pink and white crepe paper streamers and a huge honey-comb wedding bell. She could see it in her mind, and it was lovely.

Mary Frances felt better. For just a moment she had almost....

She stood and unzipped her white uniform and stepped out of it. Then she sat on the bed and pulled off her over-the-knee stockings. She dropped her slip straps from her thin shoulders and reached behind to unfasten her white bra. She shrugged it off and let it fall. It was what she did every afternoon. Then she would pull her slip straps up and throw back the candlewick bedspread and lie across the bed and rest. In the winter she pulled the folded afghan from the end of the bed over her. In the summertime, the air entered politely through the thin curtains and cooled her.

But today, as she reached down for the slip straps, she caught sight of herself in the tall mirror that swung between the two banks of drawers in the mahogany dresser. Slowly she stood and went toward it, the slip still bunched around her waist. She looked at herself. In five days she would be a married woman and her husband would see this body. Her eyes moved over her reflection and saw the dark skin stretched across bony shoulders and prominent clavicles. She let her gaze rest on her small, pointed breasts, and it lingered on the bluish veins and the delicate plumpness of the pale nipples. Then, without taking her eyes from the mirror, she pushed the slip down over her hips and stepped out of her panties. She saw hip bones that cupped a smooth, soft belly. Below it, the triangle of thick black hair was an arrow that pointed to the place that only she—and he—knew. No. Not the man she would marry.

The place inside her, where the secret had been, awakened without warning. Her eyes rose to the image of her face and she saw that there were tears on her cheeks. She wrapped her arms about herself, then lowered one hand to press the mound of soft flesh, and looking at herself, gave way to her grief. She grieved for the boy who knew her this way so briefly, so long ago. And for the girl she was, who had been carried away in joy. And for their love that came as naturally that night as breath itself, and as quickly as unexpected laughter and as deeply as pain.

She wept for their sweet young bodies revealed in the tender silver night as they undressed each other. And for the drowning ecstacy and wonder when her body enfolded his. And then her tears turned hot and bitter and she remembered how their innocence was torn away in the next moments. She turned her head to her shoulder and wept, her hands moving over her body. Slowly, the sobs quieted and the tears dried and her hands stilled, and the coin of her memory turned inexorably to the nightmare.

They had lain together, wordless after their joyful release, for only a moment before it began. Mary Frances was never sure whether she heard a sound or felt his body tense, or was blinded by the lights, for the terror and shame was an explosion. He had leapt to his feet, pulling her up and placing his body betwen hers and the tumult of coarse laughter and hoarse voices and searing light. He shielded her, making a circle of his arms and his head and folding her in it. But he was torn away, and the voices laughed and shouted. "Hey, Slats, whatcha got here? Hey, boy, give us a look! Hoo, boy, look at them little ol' tits!" And they were closer—big, wide, muscled bodies given brilliant fuzzy white-gold outlines in the headlight of the car that had coasted, silent and dark, to a stop only yards from where they lay. "Hey, the tall ones with the little tits—they're the ones that gets the hottest!"

And their hands were on her and she heard *his* voice, "Stop. No. Oh, my God, stop...."

And the taunts, "Shut up, Long Legs. Don'tcha wanna share the wealth? You already got yours, anyhow."

And his wail, "Oh, God let us go. Please stop. Stop!" and the sounds of blows, flesh on flesh, and the awful grunting and his moans.

She tried to twist away, but there were other hands behind her, holding her arms while cruel fingers twisted and pinched and tweaked her nipples and her hips and pulled at the dark, still damp hair. They stroked and felt and probed and she tried to scream but the sounds died in her throat. Terrible words sprayed against her naked body.

"Me first," came a voice. "Come on girl, get down—" and the smell of beer on the sicking mouth, and the thick hot tongue.

"Hey, man, how come you get to be first?"

"Shit, it's my car, ain't it, and my likker, and besides—"

Another voice cut over that one. "Stop. Wait. Jesus, there's a car coming. Let's get outta here."

And there were no more hands and no more fingers and no more bristly faces and...thank God, thank God...no more lights, as the motor raced and the car was gone. Mary Frances fell to the cool grass. There was a sweep of light from a second car, but it flashed over her and the car sped away.

In the darkness she lay, unable to speak, unable to cry, and she felt his hands lifting her, helping her to his car. Her clothes were placed in her hands, and trembling, she struggled into them. She lay, then, her head on the back of the car seat, her arms wrapped around her shamed body and the silent sobbing began.

Later the car moved slowly and when it stopped she opened her eyes to see that they were in front of her house. She heard the door at her side open. She felt his hands under her arms, lifting her, supporting her, helping her out. As she stood, not moving, the orchid that he had unpinned when he stopped the car in the dark, before he kissed her a lifetime ago, was placed in her hands.

At the door his fingers touched hers and she opened her eyes. His head was down and his eyes were closed. The faint light from the oval window in the door fell on his face and it was so terrible that her breath stopped. He stood, like that, for a long, long time, and then, never raising his head, he tried to speak. Twice he began, but each time his voice failed, and she never knew what he would have said.

The breeze came through the lace curtains and feathered across Mary Frances's body and she stopped her hands and shuddered out of her memories. But as she straightened her body and opened her eyes, a sudden panic rose in her throat and she whirled, her hands over her face. It was just a thought—or an emotion—unformed words, that burst through the still tender break in her heart. It trembled in her with fear and knowing. He had never come for her because he had been trapped beyond that glass wall that separated the two parts of their one being. In his secret heart, he was as bound to her as she to him. Dear God, her own heart cried, he might still come for me.

"No!" Her voice was loud and hard, and she stood straight, her hands out to push away the thoughts. "He never came and he's not coming now. It's too late."

DWAYNE

Dwayne Linfers sprawled in one of the new maple captain's chairs that sat around the new round maple table in the big new kitchen. His shirt was rumpled and his thick black hair was uncombed. He rubbed at the stubble of beard and thought about shaving. Instead, he reached for the thick coffee mug in front of him. Even the mug was cold. The morning sun came through the picture window behind him, heated his shoulders and nagged him. Time to get out and get the tractor going and tend the thirty acres along the creek.

He hadn't done it yesterday. Or the day before. Or the day before. Should have done it last week.

Slowly he unfolded the tall, thin body that the years had made muscular and strong, and took the mug to the sink to put it in with yesterday's dirty dishes. He selected a spot and placed it there, as if he were afraid of making a noise. Afraid that the sharp shards of clatter might pierce his exposed emotions and make him bleed.

When the mug was safely positioned, he lay his hands at the sides of the sink and leaned on them. He thought he would use some of the time that seemed interminable now, in staring out the window. He tried, but failed, to stop his gaze from wandering to the countertop, to the crumpled, finger-marked ivory envelope that came in the mail two weeks ago and killed a part of him. *Mr. and Mrs. Gordon Johanssen request the honour of your presence at the marriage of their friend, Miss Mary Frances Birdsong*...it said. The pain was beginning again behind his nose and eyes, and in his throat, and so he turned away and went through the kitchen door, past the shiny new Kenmore washer and dryer in the utility room, where there was plenty of room for sewing and ironing. He took his cap from a hook next to the door and stepped outside into the morning air.

As if his long limbs were too heavy to function properly, he staggered along the wide concrete sidewalk and through the gate. Then, because his habit was so strong, he turned to look back at the house. It was yellow brick and it was new and big, and it sat in the center of wide, green lawns. He thought about the thick carpets and the fully-lined drapes. He thought about the big rooms, almost empty, except for the kitchen and small back bedroom where he slept. He saw the dark green shutters that flanked the windows. And the roses and hydrangeas that marched along inside the cyclone fence that closed in the place he had built. For her. For them. His mouth pulled up on one side in a grim smile. "What gaineth a man...?" he muttered, corrupting the Biblical phrase to fit his own misery. He heard himself moan. Too late. The dream is gone. Over. Ended.

He pivoted in the gravel and went toward the old barn. Seeing it, the mirthless smile twisted his face again. His father would tremble in his grave if he could see the farm today. His father knew how you ought to run a farm. He had installed electric lights in the barn as soon as Roosevelt's REA ran the lines down the main road, but it was years later before he wired the house so Dwayne's mother could have a refrigerator and get a proper electric washing machine to replace the gasoline washer that she filled with a hose in the yard. His dad would rave at a son gone crazy when he found every possible new appliance inside the house while in the barn sat the same machinery that was there when he died, old, even then, and now kept running with rebuilt parts and baling wire.

But, Dwayne thought, his father would have to accept it, because that's how it has to be. Then he reformed the thought in past tense. That's how it *had* to be. His jaw worked and, with calloused fingers he rubbed his forehead under the visor of his cap. Too late. No more. The dream had been so real, so natural, so much the way things had to be that he had let himself be a fool. A fool!

It would have been better if he'd never come back. The pointless, directionless life he'd led all those years, seventeen years of moving from Navy base to Navy base, from sea to sea on great warships, sprawled in his bunk, reading, reading, reading—that was better than this. It would be better, easier, if he had never had the dream.

He winced, remembering how it had begun and where. He had long since put aside any guilt for the happiness that had come to him that day as he stood making polite conversation with neighbors he didn't remember, around his father's grave. Someone had said, as if she were no more important than the scores of other people they gossiped about, that poor Mary Frances Birdsong had never married. Still worked at the cafe in Cedar City, they said, and he'd felt bathed in light, as if he stood in one of the great rays of sunshine that beam down in religious paintings. He knew on that day, as though the one truth of his life had been imparted to him, that it was the same for her as it had been for him. She had waited. All the answers that he had looked for on the pages of all those books all those years, to all those questions, came to him. He knew that moment that they wouldn't be whole if they were apart, and that they couldn't have been together before because of the intensity of the awful thing that happened that night to the not-fully-formed souls of two so young. There was that joy that melded them so they shared one heart, but then the agony of what had happened next, and his terrible failure, had put a barrier of shame and humiliation between them. Had separated their bodies but not their souls. But their souls and hearts were older now. Stronger. He wanted to shout at all the unfamiliar faces around him in the old cemetery, *it's all right now. She waited.*

He had returned to the farm then, the new knowledge wrapped around him. In the following days, he devised his plan. He would build a place for her on the land that was his now. And when it was finished, he would bring her here. It would be the perfect gift, the perfect surprise. It would make it all up to her—all her years alone—and his failing her.

He had thought, in his happiness, that he could have it ready in a couple of years, but the first two years there had been nothing left over when the crops were in and the bills paid. But he'd learned everything the county agent had to teach him and he'd read the magazines and gone to the farmers' meetings and spent a painful lot of his savings on good seed and good fertilizers and hired help. And he had worked before sun-up and after sundown and seven days of each week, and the third year there was a profit. The fourth year there was more. And the fifth year he had built the house. Last year he got it ready inside and put in the yard. This year he would trade the broken-down old Ford in on a big new car, and in it, he would go and get Mary Frances.

Suddenly he caught himself. He had let himself believe again—believe that the message that came in the ivory envelope hadn't come at all. As it had a hundred times in the past days, despair packed his throat with cotton, and when he spoke, his voice, pushing past it, was hoarse. "No," he said. "No! It was all ready. Too late." His voice faded. "Too late. Too goddamned late."

He wiped at his face. He had no idea how long he had been standing before the big sliding door of the barn. He pushed it open and it bounced against the stop. Inside the dim, musty, dusty barn, he climbed on the aging tractor and pushed the starter button. Blue smoke poured from the exhaust pipe. He jammed the gears into place and the tractor backfired as he rumbled out of the barn. It jolted along the fencerows to the field beside the creek. There Dwayne stopped it, and clanking the levers, lowered the plow blades into the fertile black soil.

Eventually the sound of the engine smoothed and the clean air of the morning and the warmth of the sun and the look of the rich, moist soil beneath the tractor soothed him. He turned to look behind and saw the plows, polished blue-black by the gritty soil, leaving their long, dark, shining cylinders of earth.

He was calm. He asked himself again how he could have been so wrong. Since the day at the funeral he had believed that she would wait forever. That when he was ready, she would be there. True, he had thought when he saw that his preparations for her would take longer than he planned, that he would write to her. Night after night he sat at the kitchen table and struggled with words that would tell her what was in his heart. But his store of words, gathered from all the pages of all the books he had read, failed him. And he told himself that it didn't matter. That she would wait. He thought that she, like he himself, had no choice. He felt his stomach twist. He was wrong. He had been stupidly wrong. Somewhere inside him he had known there was a risk. But he had chosen to delude himself. He had let himself become caught up in the anticipation, the fairy tale, and he'd been unwilling to face up to the awful chance he was taking. He had brushed away the little tweaks that said, *Be careful. Don't wait too long. But it has to be perfect,* he'd argued. *Just a while longer and it will be perfect.*

Dwayne turned his face to the sky and the sun shone on his dark skin and his long straight nose and the tinges of color high on the cheekbones. *Well, Dwayne, it's perfect now. Everything's just perfect. But you're too late. You waited too long. For some reason that you don't know, and will never know, she gave up. Tomorrow she will marry someone else.* Pain burned behind his face again and he wondered if, out here where there was only him and God and the tractor, it would be all right to cry.

He bent and lay his head on his hands that gripped the bumping, lurching steering wheel of the old tractor. *Too late. I waited too long. I miscalculated.* The years lay long and dead ahead of him. His heart would go on beating and he would go on breathing in and breathing out again, but to what purpose?

His head came up and his face turned to the searing sunshine. It had been so close. Within his grasp. He had been given a second chance to salvage their one shared life. And he had failed. He had failed her again.

The paper bag crackled as Dwayne set it on the cluttered countertop. He flipped a light on and, out of the bag, took two cans of chili and a bottle of bourbon. He opened the cabinet where he kept the few cooking utensils, but there wasn't a pan to warm the chili in. He remembered, then, that he'd used the last clean one the night before.

No matter. He picked up the bottle, found a glass beside the sink, rinsed it out and went to the big round table. He slouched into a chair, rested the foot of one long leg on the knee of the other and reached out and picked up the bottle. He screwed the cap off and glugged the liquor into the glass and drank. It made him cough and he wiped his mouth with his sleeve. When he rested his hand on the table again he noticed the soil on his cuff. Unimportant. It was amazing how many of the things he thought were important a couple of weeks ago had turned out to be inconsequential. Most of all, what he looked like or smelled like.

Funny how a man could get himself so damned worked

up about something so unimportant. He squirmed and swallowed more bourbon as he thought about the way he had squandered the past seven years. Any sane person could have told him, and *would* have if he'd let anyone know what he was up to, that he was nuts. Seven years of his life given to a silly dream that was more suited to a teenage girl than to a man of forty-one. He was disgusted with himself.

Well, he'd made a lot of improvements in the place, anyway, even if the process was backwards. There was a lot more to do, but now, by God, he knew to put first things first. He needed new equipment, lots of it. He'd take the money he'd put aside for a fancy car and get a new tractor first. Next year he ought to be able to put up a new barn. Make this farm into something even his dad could have been proud of. He grinned, beginning to feel the warmth of the alcohol. "Yeah, Dad. Don't know what the hell was the matter with me. Something wrong with my heart...." He sucked in his breath and coughed, "My *head*, I mean."

He felt the weight coming down on him again and he poured more booze. After a time he noticed how light it was in the kitchen and he wanted it to be dark. He got up and turned the light off and sat down again, sliding forward on the chair, his legs stretched out in front of him. His eyes adjusted to the bluish glow that came from the light on the tall pole in the barnyard.

"That's better," he mumbled, and thought how well the glass fit his hand. "Don't need to see anything. Nothing worth seeing in here." He emptied the glass and poured it full again.

"Well, Dwayne, old boy, tomorrow's the day. She's gonna do it tomorrow and you won't have to worry any more. No, sir. You'll be set free! Ain't that just fine? Just fine!" His head went back and turned to the side and he moaned. "Ain't that just fine, Dwayne Linfers? You're a free man. After all these years...." His voice became soft and soon he was crying, the tears finding convenient creases in his face to run down. The small sounds of the crying went on for some time, then his breath came deeply and evenly and his hand loosed its grip on the glass and lay open on the table.

## MARY FRANCES BIRDSONG'S WEDDING DAY

It was six o'clock on the morning of Mary Frances Birdsong's wedding day when Clarence Peavy closed the back door of Betty Lou Hooper's house. He stood in the shadows on the steps for a few seconds, still arranging his clothes, and looked both directions. Then he walked stealthily to the alley and turned and went two blocks to the old cemetery where his car was hidden under the draping boughs of a weeping willow.

It was very early on the morning of Mary Frances Birdsong's wedding day when May rattled the top down over the fifteen-pound ham in the restaurant-size roaster. With the back of her hand, she wiped the perspiration off her forehead. She'd been in The Gormay Cafe kitchen for an hour, and the turkey was already in the oven.

At the sink May washed her hands, and as she wiped them on the damp towel, she went to the swinging door that led to the dining room and pushed it open. She smiled. The Gormay Cafe looked lovely. She and Gordie and the boys had worked late getting it ready. They had set up the pretty white lattice-work screen that Mary Frances and Clarence would stand in front of so that it made a kind of a partition between the front part of the cafe where the folding chairs were lined up for the guests, and the back where they had put three tables together to make a long reception table. The four-tier wedding cake was beautiful, and May had got a good price on it from the bakery that made the Gormay's cinnamon rolls and pies. It stood in the center of the table, on the lace cloth, with the candelabra from the church on both sides. Above the table, at the center of twisted pink and white crepe paper streamers that came from each corner of the room, was a huge paper honeycomb wedding bell.

When the ceremony was over, they'd push the lattice screen back against the wall and move the chairs back, and there would be plenty of room for the reception line and for people to move around while they ate. They could sit in the booths to visit if they wanted to—May had put a little bouquet in each booth on a lacy paper doily. Up front she'd strung ivy along the counter, and had big baskets of peonies in front of the cash register and the milk shake machine so you'd hardly even know they were there. She sighed with satisfaction. It looked beautiful.

She let the door swing shut and untied the big white apron. Even though they had worked so late doing up the cafe, she and Gordie had talked a long time after they were in bed and the lights were out. They'd talked about Mary Frances and Clarence, and Gordie had told her she ought not to worry so much, that Mary Frances was a sensible and patient woman, and Clarence wasn't so bad. And May had thought about Mary Frances being forty-one and all, and this being probably her last chance, and finally she had convinced herself that Gordie was right. She was determined to be happy for Mary Frances. It was going to turn out fine, after all.

As she went out the door and turned the key in the lock, she was looking forward to getting all ready in the pink matron-of-honor dress, and picking up Mary Frances and bringing her over here. She could hardly wait till Mary Frances saw the way they'd fixed up the cafe.

She glanced at her watch as she went down the back steps and it was six o'clock straight up. She heard a car going by on Second Street. She looked across the empty lot behind the cafe and saw it clearly. "For goodness sake," she muttered, "what on earth could Clarence be doing out at six o'clock on the morning of his own wedding day?" She stood on the bottom step for a moment. "He's just nervous, I guess. Had to get out of the house, probably."

But she felt awful again.

It was six o'clock on the morning of Mary Frances Birdsong's wedding day and Dwayne Linfers shouted as he leapt out of his bed, throwing covers onto the floor. "No!"

His heart pounded and he gasped for breath. He covered his face with his sweating hands and then took them away. Fully conscious, the details of the dream taking their places in reality, he looked down at himself. He still wore the dirty denim pants and faded blue shirt he had on when he took the bottle of bourbon to the table the night before. He had no idea when he had come to this little back room to throw himself across the tangle of sheets and quilts.

He stood straight and lifted his head and closed his eyes. The dream was still keen. It wasn't the first time he had relived that night in his dreams. Too many times it had crept into his sleep, monstrous and ugly, to cramp in his belly. Everything—feeling the explosion of light on them and knowing, instantly, what it was. Knowing he must protect her, scrambling to his feet, gathering her naked body to him, trying to shield her from the lights and the voices. And then feeling himself torn from her and held. In the dreams, as in reality, he struggled against the hands that held him while other hands reached out and touched her and hurt her. He stood helpless, in agony and shame and terror of what they would do, and he felt as though the skin and flesh had been torn from his body and the lights and sounds were acid that poured over his exposed organs. He had fought at the strong arms, but they held and he had screamed. They hit him, then, and laughed. He had been weak and impotent and helpless while they handled her. And in all the dreams before, it had ended that way.

But not this time. Not this dream that had awakened him and yanked him to his feet and made him shout. In this dream on this morning he had been strong. He had pushed them away, one by one, and there were no blows and no laughter and no taunting and no hands on her. And when he turned back to her she was standing, in her rose-colored dress with the white orchid at her shoulder, and the light of the night in her eyes. He had gone to her and he, too, was clothed, and he had held her to him and in his dream she whispered, "I love you Dwayne. I want to be with for for all of my life."

Standing there in his dirty clothes, his hair rumpled and a nasty coating on his tongue, he knew that he'd remembered that night imperfectly. He'd remembered it only as he had seen it himself. Never as it was for her. There in the morning light he knew that she had never blamed him. He saw her agonized face as she stood trembling at her door that awful night, and he knew that her suffering had been for him, as his was for her.

"Oh, you fool," he wailed at himself. "You poor damned fool! You almost gave up!"

Then he was running. In the bathroom he splashed water on his face and looked in the mirror to see the ill-kempt, unshaven bum he'd almost let himself become. He snatched a towel from the rack and said, "So much to do...." He remembered the words on the invitation: *eleven o'clock in the morning.* "So much to do."

He turned around twice then ran down the hall to a closet and took out the blue suit he'd bought a year ago. There was a spot on the lapel and it panicked him. Then he remembered the can of carbon tetrachloride in the barn. He yanked the coat off the hanger and ran to the barn, and when the spot was cleaned off, he ran back to the house and put it back on the hanger, and then outside to hang it on the clothesline so the odor would evaporate.

Then he dashed to the kitchen. So much to do. So much to do. All those dirty dishes and pots and pans had to be cleaned up and everything wiped down, and the kitchen floor and the floor of the utility room mopped. All the carpets had to be vacuumed. And the bathrooms checked. And the big bed made.

Two and a half hours later he stood in the center of the kitchen, panting, and saw that one more thing was needed. He ran to the yard, and with his pocket knife, cut roses and hydrangeas and took them to the kitchen. He found a water glass and filled it and stuffed the stems of the flowers into it and set it in the middle of the round maple table.

"Eight thirty," he whispered, and ran to the bathroom. When he was clean, he found a white shirt and a dark blue tie and dressed in the dark blue suit. He looked at himself in the mirror and his heart jumped when he saw a man whose hair was graying. Who had lines in his face. She would remember only the boy. He was panicky again. He had not seen her, either, for twenty-two years, but she was forever beautiful to him, and in his heart he knew he would be the same to her as he was so long ago.

He found his wallet and keys in the back room beside the bed and half-ran out to the old Ford in the graveled space between the barn and the cyclone fence around the yard. He brushed something off the car seat, wishing it could be different. Wishing he had the big new car for her. But it had to be this way. He put the key in the ignition and turned it. There was a rattling that became a grinding that became a low, dying growl that became a terrible silence.

It was nine o'clock on the morning of Mary Frances Birdsong's wedding day and she stood before the window, staring through the lace curtains where the sun came through and dappled the hands that were clasped in front of her. She was very, very tired, because she had been at the window almost all through the night. Three times she had gone to the bed and lay down and stared at the ceiling where the streetlight cast a gold parallelogram through the window, and three times she had found herself again at the window, not knowing when she went there.

She'd watched the black of the night change to the pearl gray of the dawn and the pink gold of the sunrise, and still she stood. Just two hours now, and she would be married. She would be a good wife. She would see that Clarence was not unhappy, and she wouldn't let herself be unhappy, either. She tried not to remember that through the long night she had kept seeing her life as a many-pointed star that was about to have all of its bright points broken off. And when she couldn't help seeing it that way, she told herself that if the points were gone, then the deep chasms between them would be gone, too, and so, all in all, it would be a good thing.

With a deep sigh, Mary Frances Birdsong pulled on her robe and went down the hall to the bathroom to begin preparing herself for her wedding.

## THE WEDDING

The minute hand on the Coca Cola clock ticked forward and it was eleven o'clock on Mary Frances Birdsong's wedding day. The Reverend Krenk smiled the solemn smile that served for funerals as well as weddings, and said, "Now. If you'll just stand here, Mary Frances, with May beside you. And you, Mister Peavy, over here with Gordon...." He placed them, then stepped back and checked their positions through his bifocals. "Yes. Yes."

May smoothed the pink matron-of-honor dress over her hips and tipped her head down to sniff her corsage of pink rosebuds. She looked out over the crowd sitting in the rows of chairs the boys had set up. They were all there. The mayor and his wife, Mary Frances's neighbors, the other two girls who worked at the cafe. Even Betty Lou Hooper was there and May wished she'd just thrown that invitation away before she ever got to the post office with it. Betty Lou had on a kelly green dress that was out of place not just because of the color, but because it was cut way down past where her cleavage started.

Everybody they had invited was there. Except one. Dwayne Linfers hadn't even sent a card and May was relieved by that. But for some reason she was uneasy. About something. Not Dwayne Linfers. It started when she saw Clarence in his car on Second Street so early that morning. It nagged at her—where could he have been? She'd be glad when the wedding was underway, then maybe she would just relax.

She stole a glance at Mary Frances beside her. She looked a little better. When May picked her up at her house half an hour ago, Mary Frances had been as pale as skimmed milk. After they got to the cafe, May took her to the restroom and helped her touch up her make-up with some rouge and mascara she had in her purse, and now she looked a little more like a bride ought to. May could see, though, that the satin-back crepe dress hung loose on Mary Frances, and she wondered if she had been losing weight again. She reached out and took her hand and it was trembling.

"You okay, honey?" she whispered.

Mary Frances looked down at her and said, "Uh huh." But the corners of her mouth were quivering, and there was a soft, damp look around her eyes. The nosegay of white roses and stephanotis that she held shook. But, May thought, every girl is nervous on her wedding day. Shoot, I was shaking like a quaking aspen when I married Gordie.

"Are we ready?" Reverend Krenk's voice was dry.

May leaned forward to look around Mary Frances at Jimmy who stood off at the side. She nodded her head and he disappeared into the kitchen. In a few seconds, the music of the wedding march from the *Songs of the Universe* album came drifting out. May gave Mary Frances one more look. She was standing like a porcelain doll, her eyes not focused on anything.

Reverend Krenk began the ceremony. "We are gathered here...."

Everybody was quiet, the women all sitting up straight, their heads tipped to the side a little, and smiles on their faces. In the second row the girl who worked Thursdays at the cafe wiped at her eyes with a Kleenex. Mary Frances's nosegay was shaking so hard May was afraid the flowers would begin to drop out. May moved a little closer to her so their arms touched. Clarence cleared his throat, like he was about to choke, and on the other side of him, Gordie shuffled his feet in his new shoes.

But the ceremony was going forward. May heard the clock and thought, *just seconds now. Just seconds and it will be done. Mary Frances will be a married woman.* The preacher droned on, "...if any man has reason...."

Then everything went to pieces at once. Just as Mary Frances whirled and buried her face in May's shoulder, moaning, "Oh, May, I can't. I can't," Betty Lou Hooper stood up in the fourth row and said so loud you could hear it at the county seat, "*I* have!" She started for Clarence, and on the way she ran into the preacher and knocked his glasses off. Clarence backed into the latticework screen and it teetered and tipped over. Gordie caught it just before it went all the way down and slapped it back into place. Over all that confusion came a banging and popping and roaring outside in the street. Half the people stood up to look out, and several chairs turned over as a rusted old tractor slammed into the curb, one front wheel wobbling up on the sidewalk. A tall thin man in a dark blue suit vaulted from the seat and burst through the door.

"Stop," he shouted. "Wait!"

Mary Frances turned at the sound of the voice and went so pale her rouge looked like clown make-up. The white roses and stephanotis dropped to the floor and her hand went to her throat.

The tall man was forcing himself through, pushing people aside, stepping over the fallen chairs. May gasped and muttered, "My God, is that...? Oh, my God, it is!"

He was in front of Mary Frances by that time, and May heard her breathe his name. "Dwayne?"

Dwayne took Mary Frances's hands in his. "Mary Frances," he said, an expression of panic in his eyes, "Mary Frances, you can't."

"I know. I know." There was a smile of such quiet happiness on Mary Frances's face that May began to cry and then to laugh through her crying. Mary Frances and Dwayne stood looking into each other's eyes as if there was nothing and no one else in the whole world. May was sure Mary Frances didn't see Betty Lou dragging Clarence through the door. Reverend Krenk was feeling around on the floor for his glasses.

Slowly a silence took over the room. All the people stood staring at Mary Frances and Dwayne. Such a warmth and light radiated from the two of them that it was as if the sun was shining inside The Gormay Cafe. It was a long time before a couple of men began to grin self-consciously, and someone in the back giggled.

Dwayne pulled Mary Frances's arm through his and turned to face the people. "I'm sorry I was so late. But," he looked at Reverend Krenk who was still trying to hang his glasses on his ears or nose, and said, "I think we can get on with the ceremony now."

The preacher sputtered and caught his glasses as they fell again. "Who is this man? I don't think...this isn't the way it's supposed to be." But he seemed to be hypnotized by the authority and purpose in Dwayne's intense blue eyes. He blinked and said, "Well. Well." Altogether, he said it five times, and then mumbled, "Yes. Yes, I suppose for now...."

"Then you may proceed," Dwayne said.

When Reverend Krenk said, "I pronounce you man and wife," Dwayne wrapped his long arms around Mary Frances and she turned her glowing face up to him and they kissed. They kissed so long that the crowd began to titter and buzz. Finally they parted and turned to the people. Everybody came up to them, but shyly, because they looked so tall and majestic, and their happiness seemed almost too much for The Gormay Cafe to hold.

Then Dwayne took Mary Frances's arm and led her through the crowd and out the door. He lifted her up beside him on the tractor seat that wouldn't have been big enough except for how close he held her. Jimmy and Bobby pushed and shoved their way through the people and as the tractor engine backfired and puffed smoke, they tied a string of tin cans and old shoes to the raised plow blades.

May worked her way to Mary Frances, and just as the tractor began to move, she reached up and took her hand. Mary Frances turned her face away from her husband and looked down at her and May gasped. It was the Mary Frances of twenty-two years ago. The Mary Frances of the dusty rose dress and the white orchid. May choked on a happy sob. Olivia de Haviland was never so beautiful.

# About the Author

In 1952, a very young mother put on her good Navy blue dress, red felt hat and white gloves, and went to the offices of The Lebanon Express, a newspaper that published twice a week in her small town. She insisted she could write, and even though she had little proof of that, the publisher gave her the opportunity to try. In the next half-century, Maggie Morgan Doran raised two daughters and a son while she wrote advertising copy, obituaries, news stories, public relations pieces, ran her own advertising agency, founded and published industrial magazines and finally, when it was no longer necessary to write for money, sat down to write fiction. She soon found that short stories were her strength. Her characters are based on the people she'd known from her early childhood in the oil field shacks of Dust Bowl Oklahoma, through professional years in the Willamette Valley of Oregon, and then a decade on the island of Maui. She now lives near Tucson, Arizona, with her cats, Thelma and Louise.